LOVE BITES

'I tell you one thing, Mum, now we're on our own we must start to think about organising our social life. I look to you to wheel on some tasty eligibles.'

'Who for? You or me? Cheeky thing!'

'Does it matter? We'll share them out – there's nothing wrong in having a pool of men for us to pick and choose from, is there?'

Molly Parkin, ex-fashion editor of *Nova*, *Harper's Bazaar* and *The Sunday Times*, is one of Britain's most beautifully outrageous ladies. She now has nine novels and a volume of poetry to her name, and has recently completed her first original screenplay and a stage play.

LOVE BITES

Molly Parkin

A STAR BOOK
published by
the Paperback Division of
W. H. ALLEN & Co. Plc

A Star Book
Published in 1983
by the Paperback Division of
W. H. Allen & Co. Plc
44 Hill Street, London W1X 8LB

Reprinted 1987

First published in Great Britain by
W. H. Allen & Co. Plc in 1982

Copyright © Molly Parkin 1982

Printed and bound in Great Britain by
Anchor Brendon Ltd, Tiptree, Essex

ISBN 0 352 31223 8

For Sarah and Sophie,
their loyalty and love

One

'This is our mother,' says Spring, introducing me to the millionaire.

'Poor thing's suffering a hellish hangover,' adds Scarlett, my other daughter. Both girls link their arms in mine, gestures of affection. Spring stands, tall and bare-breasted, bronzed skin glossy with sun oil. Her naturally blonde cropped hairstyle, bleached albino this past two weeks of Italian weather, provides an incongruously boyish contrast to her seductive curves. Scarlett, younger, and shorter like me, eschews topless sunbathing on sexist grounds. Though her breasts are equally as voluptuous as her sister's, she denies the arousing sight of them naked to the sly eyes surrounding the Hotel Excelsior pool. She has just been swimming. Her sleek scarlet and black costume, fashioned in fifties style, clings to her figure and emphasises the smallness of her waist. Her straight raven pageboy falls over her face, still wet. She towels it dry with her free hand.

I follow the gaze of the millionaire man, interested to see which of my two sirens attracts him most. A difficult choice, decided only by taste and preference.

But his eyes have fastened upon mine.

'Congratulations,' he says, extending his hand.

'On my daughters? Thank you.' He couldn't be congratulating me on my hangover. Unless the excessive extent of today's self-induced suffering qualified me for instant entry to the *Guinness Book of Records*. Surpassing hitherto standards held in breaking the pain barrier.

I ignore his outstretched fingers, knowing that if I offer my own, their violent shake might cause us both to lose balance. So instead I force my stiff, muscle-bound mouth into a semblance of a smile. The grotesque leer of a gargoyle, a demon drilling at every nerve. When I return to London I shall join Alcoholics Anonymous, or resolve never to touch 'peasant rough red' again. Just stick with my civilised champagne habit.

'Congratulations to you on your lovely daughters, and congratulations to your daughters on their beautiful mother. My pleasure at meeting you now is only marred by the information imparted to me this morning by your daughters that you are due to depart Venice today. Does that really mean all three of you? Can't I persuade you to stay?'

Both girls giggle at me, their green eyes shiny and mischeivous with mock greed. The green eyes which they have inherited from me, together with the high cheekbones and full top and lower lip. Just as I was blessed enough to inherit these same bonuses from my own mother. Except that, at twenty-three and twenty, Spring and Scarlett's radiant splendours are enchantingly unselfconscious, without the aids of artifice. They cast their spells carelessly, never really concerned at the response. In the same way that my mother, now almost eighty, takes her beauty for granted. Wearing it like one of her gossamer shawls, faded with age. Fragile, almost to the point of extinction, yet all the more exquisite for that.

But I am trapped between these two generations, me in my middle years. Incapable of and unwilling to compete with the unsullied bloom of youth, yet mulishly reluctant to accommodate the maturing process – my inevitable oncoming matronliness – with the proper dignity. I am that most reckless, ridiculous, randy, and emotionally irresponsible of human creatures: the menopausal woman.

Older female friends tell me that when I cease to menstruate I shall feel better.

'Better?' I say back to them, 'In what way better?'

'Calmer. There comes a kind of acceptance. A harmony between the mind and the body and the emotions. The sexual drive diminishes.'

'And that's what you think of as better? That's what I'm meant to be looking forward to?' I roll my eyes until only the whites are showing.

8

'Less bother all round at our age,' they reply, 'when you can't get what you want anyway.'

'Speak for yourself,' I sniff back. 'I'm doing all right. If I can't get what I want, that's not who I go for. There are plenty of people around that no-one else would dream of fucking. That's what I settle for now, the left-overs, all the dross. Human debris. I specialise in it.'

'But you must have *some* standards!'

'I honestly don't see why. If I weren't so aware of the wrath of my dentist, and the cost of re-capping, I'd gnash my teeth in vexation at all the offers I've turned down by clinging to so-called standards. I used to draw up whole lists of them when I was seventeen. No-one old (over twenty-four). No-one married. Or engaged (especially if engaged to one of my best friends). No-one with pimples and boils (and unpressed blackheads around the nose). No-one with an accent as common as my own. No-one who wanted me to take off my roll-on (before even asking me to marry them). No-one who didn't go to chapel every Sunday. No-one who drank (even cider). And as little as a year later, by which time I was an art student, I'd done all of those things. Gone out with everyone on the list. And all I can think of now is how much time before that I'd wasted. Now that I'm so much older I view time as a precious commodity, and standards as self-imposed deceptions.'

'You come to terms with life, that's what happens when the curse stops. It becomes easier with the opposite sex, you no longer worry whether they find you attractive. The desire for conquests just disappears.'

'Yes, well, you speak from the safe harbour of a home with a husband in it. A hot cock to hand, whenever you want it – if you'll pardon my crudeness. For we single girls it has to be a case of "seek and ye shall find".'

But my answer only brings sighs, sighs of exasperation. The decision to end my second marriage didn't please some of my friends.

'But, Eve,' they countered to me on the telephone, 'you and Adam go so well together. You're such a terrific couple.'

'We were. But not any more. It's been eleven years, after

9

all, and the thing's ground to a halt. Perfectly possible to accept that, I should have said. My first marriage lasted eleven years too – interesting – I must be an eleven-year sprinter.'

'But you were younger then, when you divorced Henry. Easier to find someone else.'

'What has finding someone else got to do with it? Who says that I won't enjoy being on my own?' I tried not to sound belligerent, but there was something about their attitude that I found vaguely insulting. As if they were viewing me as a pitiable victim in all this. Whereas at that early stage in the divorce proceedings I was aflush with self-congratulation, buoyant in the belief that everything was for the best. I hadn't started to miss married life then. I really thought that I'd stopped loving Adam.

He was the one who had actually brought matters to a head, in our rooms at the Chelsea Arts Club where we were staying at the time. We'd been back from the States for something like two weeks, after a whole year of living in New York. In that two weeks we had shared five lovers. A young couple into group sex (something we'd taken up in New York). A French student, lesbian (coolly anti-Adam). An exotic art student, homosexual (barely tolerant of me). And a beautiful Ingrid Bergman type, teenage, even younger than Scarlett. I'd had misgivings over than one, so much so that it had almost led to a quarrel with Adam.

'She's not really keen on this threesome with us, Adam. I feel as if we're taking advantage of her.'

'Of her what? Her inexperience?' He'd laughed. Coldly, it seemed to me. 'Don't worry. She's been around, that one. Not as innocent as she makes out.'

'Not with men, maybe. But I'm talking about me.'

'You, Eve! She *adores* you! You're everything that she wants to be. Glamorous. Sophisticated. Successful. A celebrity. She's seen you on TV. She's read all your books. She's a star-fucker, you can see it a mile off. You should be thankful that your fame is actually working for you, pulling all manner of people into our bed, instead of maundering on about morality. I tell you something, I know that I wouldn't stand a chance with her if it wasn't for you.'

'You'd stand a chance with anyone, Adam.' I was bolstering his sexual pride.

'I used to think so, before I married you. But I've lost the touch, getting too old in the tooth.'

'You! What about me!' Me, seven years his senior.

'For some reason it doesn't apply to you. You're just one of those women. You're a witch, you cast spells. Your age will never affect that. I wouldn't have believed it unless I'd seen it this past year. I honestly think that you could pull whoever you want. Hardly fair, but that's how it is.' His compliment hung between us, spiced with a special bitterness.

The night with the girl was the most painful of our marriage. We'd taken her out. Champagne at Langan's Brasserie, arriving a little high from the shared snort of coke in the back of the cab. But the girl was over-excited already. Whilst waiting for the taxi in the Kings Road, she'd sighted one of her idols. An actor, an old friend of mine, whose career had burgeoned during our sojourn in the United States. He was now starring in his own television series. I'd known him between my marriages, before I'd even met Adam. We'd been to bed together three or four times, but things were nipped in the bud by my whirlwind romance with Adam. The two had always been distant with each other.

'Look, look who that is!' The girl wriggled by my side, pointing.

'Christ, that little shit,' groaned Adam. 'No doubt he'll come salivating all over you.' His glance at me was accusing, though there had been a time when he would have found it amusing to possess a person this much admired by other men. Knowing that he had the upper hand, perhaps. Now, and especially lately, he wasn't quite so sure and viewed these attentions to me as more of a threat to himself. To our marriage and what was laughingly left of it.

'Oh, do you know him? I'd *love* to meet him.' The girl spoke in a breathy whisper. I sympathised with her, understanding so well the heady thrill of coming face to face with the famous. Even envying her naïveté, wondering how long it was since I'd felt like that. Aglow, instead of calm and faintly cynical.

The actor had spotted me, bounding across the busy street to embrace me in a bear-hug. It went on fractionally too long, so that my pleasure at seeing this old friend (and lover) was marred by Adam's scowl over his shoulder. They shook hands, the two of them, and I introduced the young girl. But the actor was only intent on me, wanting to know my telephone number now that we were back in London.

'You needn't have given it. Not to that turd, that's the last thing we want – him on our backs.' Adam remained disgruntled until our arrival at Langan's. Even the coke failed to cancel out his displeasure.

'Hardly seductive, your behaviour,' I whispered as the girl put her coat in the cloakroom. 'I don't think this kid goes for the strong silent type. And who could blame her, indeed.'

'Well, since seduction is so obviously your department, I leave the balls in your court, Eve.'

'Probably wisest, as you're so obviously lacking any yourself, old boy.' We gave each other a brilliant smile, disguising from the rest of the world the murderous light in the exchange of our glances. The girl came back in the middle of it.

'It's wonderful, being with you two.' She took hold of first my hand, then of Adam's, sighing contentedly. 'You're so happy together, it spills over on everyone. Thank you for asking me out.'

'Our pleasure. Isn't it, Eve?'

'Our *immense* pleasure, wouldn't you say, Adam?' But what I was thinking as I looked at the girl's shining eyes – 'a lamb to the slaughter'. It was the slaughters which were beginning to sicken me.

The girl was very drunk by the end of dinner, dizzy with delight at the droves of household names she had managed to meet. All friends of ours, eager to buy us welcome-back drinks. We three were the last to leave the restaurant.

'Is she going to be any good to us tonight?' The girl had fallen asleep on the table, her hair was trailing in her half-full cup of black coffee. Adam didn't even bother to lower

12

his voice.

'What do you mean, "any good" to us?' I rescued the trailing hair, deliberately choosing not to understand what he meant. Knowing perfectly well.

'This inebriate lump. Worth it, do you think? Or a total write-off? Pretty expensive for no returns, have you seen the size of this bill? Most of it's booze, down her eager gullet. Still, makes a change from you pouring it down yours. You've managed to stay commendably sober tonight, I must say. Probably turn all maternal in a moment and suggest seeing the child home to her own little bed, meaning I'll end up with bugger all.'

Bugger all, except me. When did that cease being enough? I stood up and started shaking the girl gently by the shoulder, thinking of my two, Spring and Scarlett. Hoping that neither of them would ever be caught in a situation such as this.

'We'll take her back with us. I don't know where she lives anyway.' But I didn't look at Adam as I said it, aware of what the expression would be on his face. Mean triumph, he'd got his own way. Again.

Her body was solid with puppy-fat, white and smooth as a hard-boiled egg after the shell's been removed. It seemed to invite the slow bites that Adam chose to bestow, once I'd removed all her clothing and lain her on our bed. I sat beside them on the mattress, smoking a cigarette, a brandy in my hand. Just watching. Watching the love-making skills of my husband. Not jealous, not any more, seeing him with someone else. Sharing what once was solely mine. I'd gone through all that. Nor aroused. Simply interested, as a fellow surgeon might be, studying the brilliant technical expertise of a colleague at work. For this was not a straightforward operation. The patient was unconscious, yes. Blotto, completely comatose. The trick was to seduce her from her alcoholic slumber, awake her sexual attention in the hope of some (however minimal) participation. It was a challenge to Adam, one which I'd been witness to scores of times this past year. I'd never yet seen him fail – except once, with Puck. My beautiful Puck. The boy in our brief and unhappy *ménage-à-trois*, whose

13

love for me I'd betrayed by leaving him behind in New York. To sustain this sham of a marriage with Adam.

'Had you thought of getting undressed, Eve – or will you be huddling there all night swigging brandy and blowing your odious smoke?'

Defiance drummed on my tongue. 'I might do.' I said, and blew some more smoke. Straight into his open mouth, just as he'd been about to start sucking the girl's nipple.

But this was going too far. I knew it as soon as he started to rise from the bed, his handsome brow lowered, his expression familiarly menacing.

'Just joking, my darling.' I stubbed my cigarette, slid out of my clothes, downed my drink, and swooped upon the girl. All within seconds, to avert what I knew could have been an ugly situation. It would have made no difference to Adam, there being someone else present. Hitting me, pulping me into bruised pieces.

'Now, where do you want me to start, Adam? I await your instructions.' Try as I might I couldn't control the mockery in my voice. I must be a masochist, I thought, to taunt him this much. To invite his aggression and then to whine when it erupts. So I bent forward slowly, face averted from him, and took the nipple that he had been about to suck into my own mouth. And with my free fingers I began tracing around the girl's exquisite Ingrid Bergman lips. Her body, beneath mine, began stirring.

For the next fifteen minutes I warmed to my task (I'd stolen a look at my wristwatch when I'd started, and again when I'd rolled over to let Adam take command). The girl was a natural, responsive and warm. She writhed with pleasure, but languorously like a snake in the sun. She moaned constantly, small cooing sounds contained deep in her throat. And when she opened her wet lips wide, as if to pierce the loaded night-silence with shrill screams (giving me a small frisson, fearing for the peace of our fellow residents), all she gave was a series of sighs. The grateful gasps of a young child confronted with gifts.

Stroking her parted thighs, I paused for a moment, preparing her for Adam. Making certain that she'd reached the peak where penetration was all that could please her. I

14

imagined her longing for his penis, his plunge into her pulsating parts. But my pause had made her impatient, she pulled urgently at my fingers and forced them inside. Hard and high. Buckling convulsively as I contacted her inner flesh, pushing her body down so that my fingers should feel further. Then bending, her heavy breasts brushing my own, to cover my mouth with passionate kisses . . .

I kissed her, but not for long. As soon as I decently could I tore my face away to replace it with Adam's, guiding the two together. She couldn't tell by this time who she was kissing, nor probably would she have known that now Adam's penis had eased inside her. Still very drunk, she was nevertheless transported into a sensual other-worldliness. An outer-space where all that mattered was gratification. I no longer had any part to play in the proceedings.

Later, much later (it seemed like a month, gazing bleakly out at the moonlit gardens, but must have been less than an hour), I crept, shivering, back into the bed, putting out the lights on the low table. They were both asleep, lying separately, away from each other. Adam was snoring, sprawled on his back, but feeling my naked and familiar body along-side his own he turned over to enclose me. The way we always slept, fitting together like spoons, my back to his front. Holding hands all through the night, fearful lest one of us should lose the other. Searching, in sleepy panic, for that same hand, whenever we lost contact through the threshing of a nightmare. Or when one of us arose to relieve our bladder. It was the part of our marriage which had remained pure and unsullied and still perfect, the sleeping together. The mutual soothing of our slumbering skin. And I thought of that then, as I drifted into a dream. Then I stopped thinking at all.

When I woke up, Adam was on top of me, rubbing his erection between my breasts. Breasts which he had pressed close together, in order to produce a firm passage through which his penis might pass, emerging at the top to reach the tip of my chin. Inclining my head and stretching out with my tongue, I licked the smooth glans and tasted, through my sleepiness, a salty secretion. The room was still

15

in darkness, I had no idea how long I must have been dreaming. Or even whether this wasn't still a part of my dream, except that the reality of it hit me as soon as Adam started whispering.

'Your breasts are so beautiful. So young and so firm. It's been years since I've held such a body as yours. You're so desirable. I wanted you the very first moment I saw you. I want you now. I want you to kiss my cock with your wonderful mouth. Will you do that – will you come on top of me? Make love to me, please . . . fuck me . . . go on . . . yes . . . fuck me . . . oh, you're so wet . . . you move so well . . .'

He thought I was the girl. If there had been any doubt in my mind at the start of his whisperings, there was only certainty now. He breathed her name into my open mouth over and over again. But I was on top of him by this time, riding his rigid dick as if it were a bucking bronco. Mercilessly now, I brought him to orgasm. And then, driven on by demon emotions in myself (laced by an erotic intensity I had rarely experienced ever before, with anyone), I refused him any rest. Before his still engorged penis had a chance to dwindle inside me, I started again. Rhythmically sliding up and down on him, tongue-ing his nipples, licking his lips, searching out and stroking every erogenous zone of the body I'd learnt to please over the years. And exciting myself too, perversely, in the midst of my pain. Until he could come no more . . .

'That was me.' I whispered into his exhausted ear. It was the first time that I'd uttered a word.

But it was dark and neither of us could see if the other's eyes were open or not.

'You want me to switch on the lamp?' I didn't wait for his answer. The soft light filtered over us both, revealing the inert girl lying on the far side of the bed. She'd slept through it all, or perhaps had chosen to pretend she had.

'You? All along! Eve.'

We stared at each other, satiated of our lust, yet still tingling with it. Behind my eyes I felt tears gathering, threatening to fall as Adam gathered me in his arms. Tenderly at first and then with increasing force. I struggled to

16

turn off the light, not bearing to see the expression on his grieving face.

'Eve, oh, my darling . . . what are we doing to each other. We love one another so much that it's going to destroy us. I can't bear it, can you . . .'

Not, I thought to myself, for very much longer. No.

Two

My mother's visit to London was a mistake. I'd known that it would be, but we hadn't seen each other for so long and I'd missed her, living over in New York. Really missed her, like missing Spring and Scarlett. Though they had flown over for separate holidays with their boyfriends, my mother was too nervous even to contemplate the journey. She said that she was too old, too frail. And besides, she didn't want to die in a foreign country.

'You won't die, Mama,' I'd said to her on the transatlantic telephone, ignoring Adam's gesticulations at his watch and how much this call would be costing. 'Honestly, Mama, they fly them over in wheelchairs now, people much older than you. We've seen them on the planes. And they're given absolute priority, they're whizzed through immigration and customs. No waiting around like the rest of us, really!'

'What about when they want to go though?' A stubborn note had crept in.

'Go? To where they're going, you mean? Well, they're usually being met by a relative, by their sons and daughters and grandchildren. Which is the reason for their visit in the first place.'

'Don't be so silly, Eve, I know that. I'm not senile, not yet. I mean what if they want *to go* on the plane, these people in their wheelchairs? Bit awkward, isn't it? That's what I'm saying.'

'Oh – go to the lavatory? Ah well . . .' she had me stumped. I couldn't for the life of me think what the answer was. But there must be an answer, of course.

'Adam,' I'd asked him after I'd finished the call to my mother, 'you profess to know everything. Tell me what happens when those elderly people that we see on aeroplanes, the ones that have to be taken off in wheel-chairs . . .'

He'd interrupted me. 'Spare me this discussion, Eve, there's an angel. You know my abhorrence of the aged. We don't have to share your indulgent preoccupation with geriatrics.'

'I shall persist with my usual dignity and ignore your callous comments. I need to know for my mother. She's concerned as to how they relieve themselves on the flight, should the need arise.'

'Oh, that's no problem. The cabin staff simply allow the old trouts to void their bowels whenever they wish. Then serve up the end result for the rest of the passengers to eat. You've always said that those snacks taste like so much shit – there's your answer. Next question, please?'

She never did come to see us, steadfastly refused. She'd been to the United States of America, she said, with me and the children, when they were younger. And she'd enjoyed it then, but once was enough. Besides, she'd heard of the violence. How young thugs would do anything for a bit of money, cutting fingers off women's hands to get hold of their rings. And since her wedding ring was Welsh gold, rarer than any other gold, and her engagement ring had a diamond in it, she'd be a sitting duck on the streets. She didn't fancy returning fingerless to Wales.

'I'll fly over, instead, and see you, Mama.' And I had done just that, mixing business with pleasure.

'Mixing business with duty, you mean, Eve.' Adam continued to regard my closeness to my mother with the same scepticism he'd shown from the very start. 'You honestly mean to tell me that you, a grown woman, have to ring your mother every day! I don't believe it, you're joking, surely!'

'I don't *have* to. I choose to, there is a world of difference. Just because you've only seen your mother once, and then at your father's funeral, since you left home at seven-teen . . .'

But he'd refused to discuss his own mother, he had no interest in doing so. All I had to understand was that this ridiculous ringing of mine had to stop. Otherwise we would have to reappraise our own relationship. He could take on Spring and Scarlett, he could be a father to them, but he was damned if he was going to be a loving son-in-law when he'd always loathed being a son.

We worked it out, but uneasily. I rang my mother from the office, instead of ringing her from home. So that Adam never really realised that I'd never given up the daily habit. I couldn't have given it up, it wouldn't have been worth it. Nothing to do with my conscience, nothing like that. But I could picture her waiting, lonely and alone since my father's death, waiting for my calls. Reassuring her that someone cared, someone apart from my sister, who lived close by. Showing that I hadn't forgotten all the sacrifices she'd made in the hopes that one day I would achieve my present success. So, all right, as Adam said, I hadn't managed to cut the umbilical cord. And if I wasn't careful I'd end up doing the same to Spring and Scarlett when they grew up and wanted to get away. I'd 'got away' from my mother, but I actually enjoyed the bond between us. I'd do anything to make sure that it was never broken. Even (though only I understood this in the secret part of my soul) if it meant parting with Adam. After all, I had loved a succession of men in my life. But there would only ever be one mother.

I'd made the mistake when we were leaving New York for good, coming back to live in London again, of saying how relieved I was to think that now I'd be in the same country as my mother when she died.

'I know you can't understand it, Adam, but I would never have forgiven myself if it had happened whilst we were in New York.'

He'd squeezed my hand, but was silent for a moment. When he spoke, I thought I detected despair in his voice.

'I suppose,' he said slowly, 'all that is going to start up again. You and your family. Your mother, and your sister and all your sister's children. And, of course, Spring and Scarlett. They'll all be there ringing you up and coming around. With me as the barely tolerated second husband. The outsider.'

'The outsider! Since when have you been the outsider?' I was shocked. It was the first time he'd spoken this way.

'Everything revolves around you, Adam. You know it does. You make all the decisions, who we see and where we go, and what we do. You are,' I lifted his hand to plant a sloppy kiss on it, 'you are the man of the house, my darling.'

'Don't condescend, Eve.' He pulled his hand away, roughly. 'Even I don't deserve that.'

When we got back to London I telephoned my mother from the call box at the corner of the street, not even using the telephone at the Chelsea Arts Club. For fear that Adam might come across me doing so, within an hour of our arrival. I made the pretext of having to buy some Tampax, claiming that my period was due at any time. Devious strategy, but necessary in view of our conversation, I thought.

Her voice, when it answered, was so full of delight that I nearly wept. The last time I'd seen her I'd been appalled by how much she had aged, understanding then that she'd known best. That the flight to New York would have been too taxing. Her spine appeared to have shrunk alarmingly, so that now, though never tall – always petite – she stood as high as an eleven-year-old child. Her eyes, those magnetic and hooded eyes, were filmed over with creeping cataracts. Milky marbles, still green, but opaque with no hint of their former brilliance. The chiselled cheekbones were still there and the delicately pointed chin, but the fine-pored complexion was etched with a myriad miniscule lines. As if an infant had scribbled over it with a thin-nibbed pen. Her hands, once so capable of the most intricate embroidery, the coaxing of flowers from the sourest soil, the beating of batter into the lightest puddings, the soothing of fever from the sickliest brow – these hands were now gnarled and knotted at the joints. They were ugly, they didn't work efficiently in any area any longer. She'd tried to hide them from my gaze, putting them behind her back like an ashamed child. Then bravely placing them in front of her for my inspection.

'So unsightly,' she said, frowning as if suddenly disgusted with her own self and the way that her body was beginning to let her down. Then, 'Never mind, it has to

21

happen to us all. Not a bit of good fussing.'

I'd swallowed before trusting myself to answer. What was the answer anyway?

For a moment in the call box I thought that I'd lost her. Though I'd wisely taken a stack of coins with me, at least four of them wouldn't fit in the coin slot.

'Fucking thing!' I swore savagely. You certainly knew you were back in Britain, battling with the inadequacies of the telephone system. Then it was all right. I heard her wavering next question, a repeat of the one she'd just asked.

'You're really back, then, from America – for good, is it, this time?' Anxiety laced the words.

'Yes, it's for good, Mama.' The same answer from me.

'You won't be going again. You'll be staying here now.' These were not questions, merely matter of fact statements delivered contentedly. Then as if talking to herself. 'Never going again.'

'Well,' I injected a jokey carelessness, 'I don't say I shan't be going to New York never, ever, again, Mama. I may have to go over if they publish my books there. For publicity, you know, that sort of thing.'

But I regretted it as soon as the sentence had left my lips. There was a silence at the other end. I waited, but she didn't speak.

'Mama? Are you still there?'

'When are you going, then? Soon?' There was a break in the voice. I fought down a rising desperation, feeling a knot of tension gathering in my chest.

'Don't be daft! I've only just got back. An hour ago to be exact, I rang you right away. I haven't spoken to anyone else yet, not even to Spring and Scarlett.' Guilt over this true fact, over not ringing my children first, increased the tensions spreading beneath my skin. My mother's next words added to it.

'I waited next to the telephone all day yesterday. That's when you wrote that you'd be arriving. I sat up half the night, worrying that the plane had crashed. I put the news on the wireless to see if they'd announce it. I'm not well today, with all the fretting. You should have let me know,

22

Eve. Inconsiderate. I didn't bring you up to be that.'

'I'm sorry, Mama. But there were no seats available on that flight we intended to catch. It was only a day's difference . . .' My voice trailed away. Sod it! I knew I should have let her know, I even said so to Adam. Braving his scorn, 'She's *old*, the old worry. They do. There's nothing else to do. She's almost eighty, for Christ's sake!' But I hadn't phoned, I'd left it, thinking a day didn't make that much difference.

Now she was crying, softly, weeping into the phone. 'I've missed you so much, Evie . . . every day that you've been gone. There's not a minute gone by when I wasn't thinking about you, wondering when you'd be back . . . when I was going to see you again . . .' The sobbing broke up the agonised sentences, but I allowed her to cry herself out. Engulfed now in my own numb misery, aware that the muscles at the back of my neck were interlocking into spasm. Just what I needed! Adam would be able to guess at a glance that I'd been on the phone to my mother. No-one else affected me like this.

'There, there, don't cry, Mama. Everything's all right now. I'm sorry I didn't phone about the delay. But I'm home again now, and it's going to be lovely. Hey,' my cheerful tone sounded forced to me, I prayed it wouldn't to her. 'Hey, what about your birthday! That's in two and a half weeks' time isn't it! That'll be the cause of celebration, won't it? You must come to London and I'll throw a big party for you!'

'I can't come to London. I'm not fit for the journey.' She was waiting to be cajoled.

'Not come to London – what! It's only your seventieth birthday. Seventy is nothing these days . . .'

Now I'd made her laugh. 'Get on with you, you and your seventy. I'll be eighty next year, as well you know. This'll be my seventy-ninth.'

'God, seventy-nine! Well, you don't look it, Mama. Sixty-nine, I'd have said. Honestly, you looked marvellous last time I saw you. Didn't I write and say so?'

'That was six months ago, Eve.' The voice was gentle and low. 'I've aged a lot since then. You'll see a difference, I'm

23

afraid. The legs are going, I'm . . . I'm having difficulty walking now. I . . . I have to go with a stick.'

Oh, no! Oh, no! I wailed inside. Not aged even more since last time! Don't age more, please, Mama. Stay just as you used to be. Slim and straight in your beauty. My strength. My support. If you go, who is there? Who'll understand *my* weakness? Who'll see to *my* deepest needs? I crave being a child too, not just a mother and a wife. I want somebody there who remembers when I was little. Someone who'll be as upset as me when I'm hurt . . .

'Well, Mama, that's settled then. You're coming up to stay with us for your birthday. I'll buy you a new stick as a present. Bright pink with a silver knob – how does that sound?'

Girlish giggles down the phone. 'I don't want any old silly pink stick! Peple staring! I'm ashamed enough of this one as it is, but it's ordinary wood so less people notice at least.'

'I'll have a word with Edna,' I said, love flooding my blood, releasing my tension. Mama was coming up to London. I'd get here a room close to ours in the Chelsea Arts Club. I'd give her a wonderful time to make up for my year's absence. I'd show her what a devoted daughter she had. And I'd ring my sister to arrange for her to be put on the train, so that I could meet her off it at Paddington Station.

'Yes, best to ring Edna. She's very good to me, Evie. She does everything, you know. Sees to my washing. Does the shopping. The children pop down all the time to see how I'm getting on. How are the girls, by the way? I've had nice letters, but I'd like to see them. They must be growing, must be big girls by now.'

'Spring is twenty-two, Mama. And Scarlett is nineteen. I think that they've stopped growing now.' I spoke teasingly, with affection. Our emotional scene was already in the past. Emotional blackmail, Adam would have called it. But a necessary cleansing process to reach this ease.

'Oh, you mustn't take notice of me, Eve. The memory's going, I forget everything. Just a silly old nuisance, most of the time.' But she'd said it cheerfully. 'By the way, do the

24

girls ever see that father of theirs? What's his name, that first husband of yours?'

'Henry. Yes, they're good friends. He's been a very good father, he sees them all the time.'

'Better father than husband, then. Bastard. And how's the other one? That man you're married to now. Are you still keeping him, you silly fool?'

'Adam. No, he's doing well selling paintings and lots of prints. They liked his stuff in the States. He's (I crossed my fingers to cancel out the lie) looking forward to seeing you. And Spring and Scarlett will come along. Everthing will be as it's always been. One big happy family, just as you like it.'

Walking back to Adam, away from the phone booth, I suffered a frightening sense of foreboding.

Three

So it was over, my marriage.

My second marriage had ended precisely eight hours ago, it being seven o'clock in the morning now. Adam's birthday, today. Immaculate timing. From now on, every year when his birthday came round he'd be reminded of me and of his lucky escape. If I ever talk to the pig again I shall draw that fact to his attention, with a suitable witticism. Barbed, yet blackly humorous. The sort he'd enjoy – as if I give a sparrow's shit!

It erupted last night, around eleven o'clock, immediately following the departure of Spring and Joe, and Scarlett and Sebastian. We'd spent the evening in the snooker bar of the club, drinking gently. The three men playing snooker and the girls and I just sitting gossiping.

My mother had left at tea-time. Edna and Clive had driven up for the weekend to stay with Tom, their eldest son who had just got married (and qualified as a doctor in the same week). They had Becky, my youngest niece, with them, and the three of them – my sister, brother-in-law and niece, came over to the club for tea. They were collecting my mother, in order to drive her back to Wales with them. An ideal arrangement, it seemed to me. But I'd taken the precaution of telling Adam of this plan only at the last minute, fearing a scene. The scene took place once we were on our own again.

'*Great* weekend! Well done, Eve! Thank you *very* much!'

'Glad you enjoyed it. We must do it again.' A coldness had entered my heart in preparation for this. He wouldn't hit me, I knew. There'd be no striking, followed by screwing. This wasn't the usual confrontation, this one would be plumbing the real depths, right down to rock-bottom. Our future together is in jeopardy, I remember thinking that because, as if reading my mind, Adam said it aloud.

'Our whole future together is in jeopardy, Eve. You realise that, don't you!'

I wanted to say, what future? Because I knew already that it had to be over, that I couldn't go on as we were. But that there was no going back either. Our chaotic sex life couldn't change, it would never return to there being just the two of us in our currently over-crowded bed. All that would happen from now on was what had happened back in New York. Me falling in love with Puck. And if it wasn't me falling in love again with what was intended to be a casual group-sex partner, then next time it would be Adam. Though he claimed that would never, ever, happen because he abides by behavioural rules – I frankly don't believe him. We are all of us vulnerable to everything.

And the issue to be raised, about my family, particularly my mother and my two daughters – well, that would always remain unchanged. I refused to sacrifice them. It seemed to me as simple as that. All that remained now was to say it. And so I did.

He stood, looking out of the window for a long time, gripping the white-painted sill with equally pale knuckles. Eventually he spoke.

'What it boils down to is this, isn't it really. You're fed up with me. You've had enough, you're no longer interested. I've helped you bring up the children, I've served my purpose. But now you want to be free. You don't like what I am basically, a sober and serious intellectual. A dedicated scholar, interested in staying quietly at home and reading. But,' and now he turned to face me, hostile, yet infuriatingly smug, 'but I don't care for what you've always been. A drunken loud-mouth. A bragging exhibitionist. An ageing beauty who needs to surround herself with sycophants. A shallow philistine . . .'

'No need to continue, Adam. I've got the picture.'

'Well, these are just a few of the differences between us!'

I stepped aside to avoid his venemous spit. What I had on was murder for showing every mark. But I answered him pleasantly enough.

'Interesting, Adam, how you manage, in pin-pointing

27

our differences, to make your essentials so much more infinitely flattering than mine. But now I'm going to bed.'

I stepped past him, picking up my towelling robe as I did so, and went into the adjoining room where there was a single bed. It had no pillow, so I returned and took mine from our marital bed. Correction – what had been our marital bed. Tonight, for the very first time in eleven years, I would be sleeping alone.

Adam no longer had Eve.

I lay awake the whole night. This spare room had no heater, it was cold. But I burned in the bed. I was feverish, in shock, as the realisation slowly hit me of exactly what I'd done. Or rather, what I was going to do, had to do – if either of us were to survive each other and what we'd become.

Tomorrow I'd leave Adam. I'd go away. But where would I go? Where was there to go to? I had no home any more. Both Spring and Scarlett were living with their boy-friends, though Scarlett had recently left Sebastian's place to study art up in Leeds. But they were still a couple, still together, she'd stayed with him this weekend in order to visit me and to see my mother.

I could go to my mother's, of course, she'd love nothing better. But I wasn't ready for that yet. I wasn't fit to face anyone. I hadn't yet gained control, for I knew that this icy calm (despite the burning of my body) was too brittle not to break. And when it did I had to be by myself, an animal licking its own wounds.

For the second time in my life I had come face to face with terror. A wifely terror, a womanly thing. The knowing that from now on there would be no husband around, no other half, no for-better-or-worse. Just an emptiness on the other side of a once-shared double bed. With no prospects of filling it ever again. A future doomed to a self-destructive loneliness.

I remembered this same feeling, exactly, when I'd split up with Henry. Later, much later, as the pain of our parting receded into the past and we were able to communicate as confiding and self-controlled human beings again, he'd tried to tell me how he'd felt. And it had shocked me, the similarity. Though why, I still don't know. After all, men

28

are as loving and as sensitive as women. There is never really a 'guilty party' in a divorce. The causes and effect can be placed on both sides. But a marriage is like a tree trunk, the branches being the children. When the trunk is cleaved in two, there is no longer a tree, only shafts of dead wood. Which in time becomes a rich soil, from whence fresh growths will spring.

I knew all about that. It had taken me five years after Henry to come truly alive again. It was this dying process that I was dreading now, fearing the length of the slow recuperation. If I hadn't been there before I wouldn't understand what was ahead of me.

But still it was preferable to going back.

And, I reasoned, trying to restore some order to the whirling birds in my brain, this time would surely not be as bad as the last. At least I earned money, my own money from writing. Though I had none at the moment, spending every pound as soon as it came in, assuming responsibility for the finances such as rent and food and other basics (my mother was more intuitive than I admitted to her about Adam's income). Still, the earnings were there. All it needed at this very moment was for me to finish this current novel and my agent would get the cheque. But already I'd overshot the deadline for its completion (a source of professional shame, this, for it had never happened before). And, thinking of this, I stumbled on the answer. The solution as to where I would go. I'd get on the sleeper and go to Devon, to the studio that Adam still had kept on as a storage place for his paintings down there. He surely would not object. I had, after all, paid the rent in advance here for more than a month. By which time I hoped to finish my novel, collect a lump of cash and sort out what then to do. And in the meantime Adam could stay on here, until he decided too.

All night as I lay there determining the practical details of our immediate future, since I was always the one who did that, I fastened my eyes on the foliage outside my window. There were no curtains in this room, as well as no heat, but when I'd retired to bed the street lamp had struck the rich autumnal leaves with a halo of their own. The night sky was black behind this glinting, quivering shape and I couldn't focus on anything else. It being there outside the window helped me to formulate my thoughts.

But as my future grew clearer, so did the sky itself. By dawn the image of the leaves had become reversed. Now they were dark, against the increasing lightness of the sky. And I took it to hold a special meaning for myself. That everything in life reverses upon itself, it is simply a revolving process, never what it superficially seems.

When Adam entered, naked and with an impressive erection on offer, I felt more tranquil than I had done all night.

But I refused the offer. I was polite but absolutely firm, to his disbelieving consternation.

'Christ Almighty! You're not continuing this ridiculous charade, are you? First you sleep away from me – I had a terrible night without you, tossing and turning, searching for you in the bed – I'm bloody exhausted this morning, if that satisfies you, you bitch. And now this . . . come on, take it . . .'

He tried to get into the small bed, but I swiftly nipped out at the other side, leaving him there with his penis waving disconsolately at me, like a pampered pet left out in the cold. But I was adamant in my own mind. The suffering night had shown me that I must be strong, even in the face of these fleshly temptations.

For a part of me, the loving part, longed to take Adam in my arms and say that everything was forgiven between us. Until the next time. Instead I turned and started to dress.

'It's over, Adam,' I said, matter-of-factly. 'Last night decided me, the things you said.'

He began to bluster. 'That was last night – I'd had too much to drink. I can't even remember what I said. What did I say, my darling?' He was wheedling. 'I love you, you know I love you. Come and kiss me, please kiss me. I missed you so much last night . . .'

'I'm going down to breakfast in a minute, and then I shall come back up here and pack. I'm going to the studio on the train today. I have to finish this novel. You can stay on here, the rent's all paid up, until we decide what to do.'

I looked at him directly in the eyes, my own weren't flinching. A first small, though important, victory. His own appeared glazed, he seemed to stagger before me. Then his expression changed to that of a small boy.

'Aren't you forgetting what day it is?' I ignored the appeal in his voice.

'Happy birthday.' I brushed my hair.

'What about my party tonight? You'll be there for that . . .'

'No, Adam. I'm not coming.'

'But you *must* come . . . everybody will be asking . . . it's only ever you that they want to see.'

'Well, Adam, You can't have it both ways. If your friends want to see a drunken loud-mouth, a bragging exhibition-ist, an ageing beauty who needs to be surrounded by sycophants, a shallow philistine, in short – me – I suggest that you find some different friends. Choose intellectuals and scholars this time. That should make you feel more at home.'

I couldn't eat any breakfast, none at all. I just drank the tea from the fresh pot that Clifford, the breakfast chef, made especially for me. He tut-tutted when he saw what a pathetic attempt I'd made at my toast and boiled egg.

'Not feeling ourselves, are we this morning, darling? Mm, must say you're looking a little bit peaky. Night out on the tiles, was it?' He winked and lowered his voice. 'Feeling a little bit the worse for wear myself, just between you and me, Eve. Not that any of these stuffed shirts are interested. Bunch of closet queens, if you ask yours truly.' Then he raised himself to his spindly height. 'Come and have a chat in the kitchen after, darling. Bit of a gossip, do us both good.' And he gave me another meaningful look before rushing back to the ominous smell of sizzling bacon.

'Another burnt offering on the breakfast menu this morn-ing.' The resigned upper-class voice came from behind an upheld copy of *The Times*. The neighbouring *Telegraph* shook in acknowledgement, as did other newspapers along the table. It would probably be the only spoken comment throughout breakfast, apart from murmured 'Good Morn-ings' which would greet a new entrant. This was a largely public school gathering of guests here this morning, as usual. The silence at breakfast was an unspoken rule. I, as the only female present, had no desire to break it. Especially not this morning.

I left the table before Adam had even appeared, and went straight out, intending to book my sleeping berth on the train to Devon. I only hoped that they had a vacancy. But it was October, and the seasonal rush must be over by now, with all the schools back in the autumn term again. It was free, the telephone at the top of the road. The same telephone from which I had rung my mother, inviting her to stay. Inviting the world to crumble about my ears. But I refused to dwell on that now. My immediate problem, after I'd reserved my ticket, was to decide what to do with my day. I'd have to kill an hour or so before going back to the club to collect my things. I wouldn't be taking much, my portable typewriter was the most important item, that and what little I'd already written so far of the novel. But I couldn't return there until I was certain that Adam had left for his printer's studio, where he was involved in a new project. In the meantime I'd break the news to Spring and leave a message for Scarlett at the students' hostel up in Leeds.

Spring wasn't at her flat. She must have left for the theatre already, and Joe had obviously left for his antique stall in Portobello Road.

I dialled the theatre. They had started rehearsals, Spring couldn't be disturbed. Best to ring around one o'clock when there'd be a break for lunch. I'll do that, I said, striving to keep my disappointment under control. Then I rang Scarlett's hostel. Try this evening, about nine-thirty, she'd be bound to be back by then.

Hours to go and no-one to talk to. I started walking and didn't know I was crying until I noticed that passers-by were regarding me strangely. But I walked on, not caring, on and on, street after street, until I found myself on the Embankment. There I collapsed onto a wooden bench, burying my head in my arms and howling to myself, rocking to-and-fro. Amateur dramatics, banal stuff, it crossed my mind. But so what? No-one I knew would pass me here – and if they did – I shrugged inwardly. All I'd have to tell them was the truth.

I tried to recall the past confidences of close women friends, how they'd come to terms with their marriage break-ups. Or the splitting of long relationships, which was the same situation in terms of pain. And though, God only knows, practically all my friends had gone through this at some point or other in their lives, I could only remember the case of Jenny. Jenny, whose husband had confessed to preferring men (one man in particular, with whom he'd fallen desperately in love), after she had confessed to having had a brief affair with her skiing instructor on holiday in the Swiss Alps.

'But what on earth made you tell him about such an unimportant affair?' I said 'unimportant', though I'd only been married about five years to Henry at the time and the idea of anything extra-marital then was shocking, not to say deeply sordid. 'If you hadn't let your cat out of the bag, then he wouldn't have let his. And the marriage would still be intact, with no-one any the wiser.'

She'd started crying, rocking herself just as I was doing now in my hour of distress.

'It had become *horrible* between us before the ski instructor. I only used him to bolster my own ego. And then I thought it would be better if I told Jack, just to see if making him jealous would work. But it hasn't, everything is over. He wants a divorce. I'm in despair, I still love him, you see. Guess how I spend my days, Eve? After dropping the kids off at school, I drive round and round Hyde Park. Just in circles, and I don't stop until it's time to collect them from school and go home.'

But I didn't have a car. Nor did I, any longer, have children at school. Which would at least give some sort of focus to the day. My children were grown up, they didn't need me any more to do anything for them. I couldn't even get them on the telephone, they were involved with exciting jobs and adventurous studies . . . A fresh supply of watery tears sprang forth from an inexhaustable source inside my head. At least, that's where I presumed they came from – unless humans in private grief develop a special emergency sac between their shoulders. Somewhat in the nature of the camel. Adam would know, he knew everything. Now (more tears) I'd have to invest in a copy of the *Encyclopaedia Britannica* for the answer to things. Our separation was already starting to cost me money. The bugger.

The thought of money reminded me that I hadn't yet been to the bank. I needed hard cash in the hand for taxis and suchlike. Though I paid, like everyone else I knew, with plastic money – credit-card living – I had to have real money for shopping in Devon, in that tiny place. I looked at my watch and was surprised to see that it was almost half-past twelve. Half an hour to go before I'd be able to get in touch with Spring. I must have walked for longer than I'd realised.

Jesus, I felt wretched!

Adam had left me a letter, begging me not to leave, saying we'd work it out, asking me to stay for his party, pleading for a fresh start. And leaving me two different numbers to ring. He'd be there waiting for my call. I'd written him a long letter, but on re-reading it for the third time I'd decided to tear it up and do just what he asked. That's when someone knocked on the door to say that my daughter was on the phone. Which daughter? They couldn't say. It was Scarlett, she'd gone to the hostel and just got my message.

I'd spoken to Spring already. She'd wanted to rush straight over from the theatre. 'Don't cry, Mumples,' she'd said, using a name from childhood, one that she hadn't used for many years and had only used then when she needed to feel extra-close. She and Joe were taking me out to dinner after the show that evening. Until then she was stage-managing the all-day rehearsals. Her concern made me cry further, so that I could barely find the voice even to say goodbye.

Now Scarlett's call was having the same effect. 'Poor lickle Momma.' She, too, was using a baby voice from the past. Both sweet daughters were treating me as their child – just as I had treated my own mother on the phone when she cried.

The circle was beginning to join.

Four

I was desperately in need of money. American Express had rung me up. There had been no response to the accounts they'd been sending. The amount outstanding was one thousand, seven hundred and sixty-nine pounds. And ninety-one pence! Would I kindly arrange to send the cheque in the post today, otherwise they would be forced to take legal proceedings!

I'd slumped into the nearest seat, jaw sagging and mouth dry. The adjacent mirror, never a very flattering one, reflected a quivering jelly bearing only the remotest resemblance to the human species. But I supposed it must have been me since there was no-one else in the studio.

'Look,' I was attempting a brisk tone with the impudent twerp at the other end of the line. 'Are you certain you are speaking to the right client?' I'd been going to say 'right customer', but thought it sounded too much like my small corner-shop background. Not much to do with the intricacies of high finance, the sort that this scumbag was trying to involve me in now.

'Absolutely certain. You are Eve Lynn, the novelist? Let me say how much my wife and I enjoy your work. We . . . hm . . . peruse them in bed together.'

'Thank you. That's where they are intended for, I regard them as boudoir books. I hope they raise a laugh, along with everything else?' Best get on the best side of this bugger. Nearly two bloody thousand quid!!! Christ, what the fuck did Adam think he was sodding playing at! The American Express was always his responsibility. That had been agreed from the moment we started having the card. Though the card could only be taken out in my name, me being the more potentially solvent of the two of us.

So that was it! Since the card was in my name, then

legally it was my responsibility, any outstanding debt. But Adam wouldn't do that to me, he knew my position with the bank at the moment. In fact, of the two of us, now, he was the only one in credit. His bank wouldn't allow him an overdraft, as he'd always pointed out. Whereas mine would since my agent saw to it that my overdraft was supplied with injections on a regular basis, and had been for the past nine years. Ever since I'd given up my full-time and extremely lucrative job on a top newspaper to pursue the more hazardous living as a novelist. But I'd been lucky, my books had sold well. I'd built up a readership, based on producing one novel a year. Like sausages on a factory assembly line, I saw it as that with no literary aspirations at all. And the reputation had been bolstered by television interviews, pieces written about me and my genre (comic-erotica) in newspapers and magazines. I'd created my own small industry from nothing.

But I was lacking in funds. American Express with all their millions in profits might find it hard to believe, but at this actual moment I couldn't pay their one thousand, seven hundred and sixty-nine pounds. And ninety-one pence. Though the pence I might squeeze to. The one pence.

The voice at the end of the line was patient and charming. A smooth smile with the teeth of a tiger. But I took him into my confidence, there was no other way.

'Look,' I said, 'this is the position. The paying of the American Express has always been my husband's responsibility. I assumed that he'd paid this account and it may have been an oversight. I mean that we have just returned from America.'

'I know, Ms Lynn, I read it in the papers. Welcome back to our shores, we missed you, your public.'

He was referring to a brief but salacious item in one of the gossip columns which had hinted at the sexual variety of our 'swinging' life in New York. But it was no secret, I had no shame over what we'd got up to. It had been an experiment, a widening of life's experience. What writers are meant to explore.

As soon as the item had appeared, another journalist had

rung me up, an old friend and colleague from my days in Fleet Street.

'Would you do me a favour, Eve? I'm trying to break away from the fashion page and branch out into more general stuff. I read the bit about you and Adam. Is it all true, what they are hinting at?'

'Absolutely. You know me, I never lie.'

'Well, would you let me do an interview with you? Please, an exclusive. Be a bit of a scoop for me.'

'Sure, why not. Anything to help a pal.'

And she'd done the interview, I'd spilled all the spicy beans. Just the sort of stuff that the readers of her tabloid would love. But when I'd left Adam I'd had to ring her.

'Look, kid, I'm sorry. But that interview – do you mind holding it back for a bit. Things are more complicated now. The ending has turned out differently. The slant I gave you was that group sex can strengthen the bonds in a marriage, preferable to either partner having secret affairs on the side. I still believe that it's possible – except that it hasn't worked that way with us. The ending has to be changed. It's not a happy one any more. Adam and I are splitting up.'

Being a friend, she'd sat on the interview, though I'd promised her that when the moment was right I'd let her know and she could run it. With the revised ending, of course. With other matters on my mind, concentrating on the new novel, and coming to terms with my solitary state, that conversation had flown from my memory. But the American Express man had now reminded me. There might be a way to raise instant cash after all.

'How long could you give me to pay this amount?' I oozed treacle over the phone. He'd need to swab his ear out by the time I'd finished.

'A week? How does that sound? A person in your celebrated position, coining it in, shouldn't find that too difficult. After all, it's not that large an amount.'

If it's not that large an amount why are you pestering me for instant payment? Shitface!

'I'll sort it out,' I said sweetly.

I rang the tabloid and got through to my friend.

'You can run the interview. Let's rewrite the ending, but

don't make it too much of a downer. I don't want to give "swinging" a bad name, that would be a disservice. And you can have an exclusive – only thing is, if I let you have an exclusive I think I'd like a spot of money. After all, if I wrote it myself for another newspaper, and I have been asked but I'm rushing to finish this new novel now and I can't spare the time, I would get a hefty whack. As you know, they pay highly for my services now, scarcity value.'

'Sounds reasonable, Eve. How much were you thinking of?'

'One thousand, seven hundred and sixty-nine pounds. Oh – and ninety-one pence. Please.'

It took five phone calls to agree the sum, bargaining eventually with the managing editor himself.

'Five hundred quid, Eve, that's the going rate.'

'Bollocks, mate! You're forgetting that I've been in the business.' I'd slammed down the receiver.

'We're going over the top here, because you've been in the business. We're doubling it. A thousand.'

'Stuff it up your arse!'

'We've had a board meeting on this. Top whack, one thousand, five hundred. Settled?'

'Two thousand. My price is rising in accordance with the number of phone calls you're making. Time is money to me and I'm trying to finish a novel, unlike penny-pinching, time-serving, shit-shovelling, muck-raking hacks such as you.'

'One thousand, seven hundred. No further discussion, Eve.'

'No deal. I've told you the exact amount I want. Just pay it and stop pissing about, or I'll give that to another rag, that interview. Got it!'

'We'll ring you back.' The weariness in the voice made me laugh out loud. I was actually enjoying myself now.

'One thousand, seven hundred and fifty, Eve. OK?'

'You bastards,' I chuckled. 'Oh, OK. I'm short of nineteen pounds and ninety-one pence, but I suppose I'll manage. Oh, and I expect that cheque sent express post today, so that it's in my hand by this time tomorrow. Nice dealing with you.'

'Christ – if you're looking for a career in our contracts department, there's an opening for you here any time.'

My escape to Devon had shown me who my friends were. Suddenly I seemed surrounded by warmth and goodwill, support and sincerity. But far from building me up, it had the opposite effect. I disintegrated beneath the welter of devoted phone calls. I was torn to shreds by the constant arrival of touching telegrams. I fell to pieces at the kindly pressure of a hand in the street.

I now understood how my mother had felt when my father had died. Incapable of accepting consolation even from my sister and I, his children. We, who had loved him too.

And it made me wonder which was worse. Losing a loved one through death, their physical presence removed from the world altogether. Or losing a loved one who was still alive, part of the same planet. Present as a preposterously painful reminder, present too as a possibility that what was once there might still be there. Oh, yes, I wanted to go back to Adam. I didn't say so to anyone. I didn't say it to Adam in the daily exchange of our heartbreaking letters to each other. And he didn't say it to me, not any more. Though we wanted to be with each other more than at any time during our years together, a sixth sense was in operation.

If anyone had asked me seriously how I felt about him now I would have answered, gravely, that I wished he was dead. Not from bitterness, nor malice, but because that way he would have remained totally out of reach forever.

I dreaded my return to London. Was terrified at the prospect of our first casual, social encounter. Our circles were so closely linked, the confrontation was absolutely inevitable.

So I stayed down in Devon as long as I could. The novel was going well now. I worked on it at night, right through until dawn. That way I managed to steer clear of alcohol, knowing that if I had started drinking, really drinking, the solitary sort of the serious kind, the novel wouldn't get written at all.

39

And I needed the money. After the American Express business I'd become paranoic about money. I had nightmares during the daylight hours that I would never be able to write again, that my muse might have turned in revulsion from me. And who could have blamed her, I turned in hourly revulsion of myself. From my unwashed hair. My odiferous body. My halitosis. My bloodshot eyes. My Kleenex-overblown nose. My Wellington boots. My man's toe-length mackintosh (Adam's, just to feel him enclosing me). Even the ferocious farm bull on the hillside had backed nervously at my approach on yesterday's walk. And I didn't blame him either. I'd turned into a two-legged wart-hog. I would have preferred to have been a tipsy, two-legged (or rather, legless) wart-hog, staggering across the cliff-tops, setting pandemonium amongst the screaming sea-gulls. But money was on my mind. It was as simple as that.

And also I'd promised Spring and Scarlett.

But for them I might have committed suicide. They held my sanity in shape.

They each of them rang me every single day, at pre-arranged times. I would sit by the telephone, waiting. Just like my mother waited for my calls. And if the wait was longer than five or ten minutes, I would begin to get tearful, fearing that they had forgotten. Trembling as I lifted the receiver at the ringing tone, engulfed in gratitude at the sound of their gloriously alive voices. Eager to listen to the recounting of their enlivened days. What their friends were doing, what was going on at work, the in-fighting of fellow students. How it was going in their love affairs . . .

I was doing as my mother still did with me. I was living my life through them.

When my father had died, my mother had tried to die too. As the doctor revived her she'd opened her eyes, looking into my own.

'I want to go, Eve. I do. I want to join him. I'm only coming back for love of you.'

And so it was now with Spring and Scarlett. I was not only living through them, I was also living for them. Though I wasn't much good to them at the present, I had been in the past. And I would be again in the future, when I'd mended myself. With their help.

'*Thank* you for phoning.' I said it fervently at the end of every call.

'*Silly* old boot – same time tomorrow, s'long for now . . .'

'Nighty-night, Mumples – love you a *lot* . . .'

Then, one day Adam rang. Panic pounded in my throat. I'd lost the power of speech.

'How are you, Eve?'

'Me? Me, I'm fine . . . well, I'm all right. Sort of all right . . . and . . . sort . . . of . . .AWFUL. . .'

There was no answer. Everything in the studio was shimmering, shining and shifting through a soft wall of water. It was the first time for a month that I'd heard Adam's voice. I drove a very sharp pencil into my knee to transfer the pain from my constricted throat, concentrating it elsewhere in order to clear the tubes. And I blinked so that the studio fell into focus again, then squeezed the snot from my nose enabling me to breathe once more. It was called bringing my body into line. Now all I needed was brain surgery and a nifty heart-transplant.

'I'm awful too, Eve.'

My immediate reaction was of concern. He sounded so . . . *ill*.

'But . . . but I suppose it's for the best?' As bleak as a winter wind.

Now was my chance to say no, it perhaps wasn't for the best. And I was going to say it too. But the brain surgeon hadn't shown up. There was no co-ordination between my thoughts and the tip of my tongue.

'Perhaps it is for the best, Adam . . . my darling, my darling . . . oh . . . don't . . . don't cry . . . well, yes, do cry . . . it will help you . . . I've been crying too . . . I've cried every day and every night without you . . . and it does help . . . darling, there, there . . . we'll both get better soon . . . it won't always be upsetting like this . . .'

Five

I returned to London on a Monday, my favourite day of the week. Always had been my favourite, following Sunday which I'd learned to loathe in childhood as being the day of rest. No shops open. Not allowed to play with dolls or with friends. Not allowed to read, or listen to the wireless. Just sit and contemplate the glory of the Lord, between the morning, afternoon, and evening service in the chapel. Listening to sermons, reading the scriptures, singing choral hymns. All in Welsh. And not even daring to exchange warm glances with the Pritchard boys in the next pew.

But there was a reason for returning on the Monday. Though I hadn't completed my manuscript, I was almost at the end. I would have preferred to have travelled back with the finished thing in my hand, but a television chat show was eager for me to appear on their launching programme. Diana Dors was to be the interviewer, it was her new series, similar in format to the Parkinson show. I thought it was about time that women in television were given a greater share in running things, I believed in supporting them to the hilt. And besides which I liked Diana tremendously, having met her several times. I admired her style, always had done. We got along well, I was looking forward to the show. It was just what I needed after my solitary sojourn.

In any case they were paying me well, a fat fee and all expenses. Which included my fare up from Devon. Because I was facing facts now, this was how I would have to start thinking. Planning to feather my nest for my solitary future. I had no home and I didn't imagine how long I'd be able to afford to stay on at the Chelsea Arts Club. It wasn't cheap there, though relatively inexpensive for that part of London, for Chelsea, just a hundred yards off the Kings

Road. But there were certainly cheaper places in less fashionable areas. Suburbs, like Streatham for instance, and Willesden, where I'd spent parts of my childhood. Both eyesores, both cultural arseholes of the Western world. I viewed the prospect of flat-hunting with a heavy heart.

But I wasn't thinking of that on my last evening in Devon. I was having dinner with some of my closest friends, ones who had steadfastly seen me through what I had begun to view now as the worst of my crisis (though I didn't imagine that there still might not be further crises in store). Our intention was to get disgracefully drunk.

We managed, at least, to clear part of the restaurant. The occupants of the next table left before the dessert stage. The husband approached.

'Whoops! Watch out!' We hiccupped into our glasses, grimacing grotesquely at each other.

'You'll doubtless be pleased to learn that you have ruined our silver wedding anniversary with your foul language . . .'

'Our fuckin' wot!' We squinted up at him.

'. . . and the loucheness of your conversation . . .'

'Only say'n' 'bout screwin'n'shaftin'n'suchlike.' We widened our rolling eyes in innocence at his accusations, unreasonable as they obviously were.

'And as for you,' he was looking at me now, singling me out. 'If you call yourself a lady, you are widely off the mark. I've never heard such a loud-mouth . . .'

I sobered up instantly, or felt as if I had.

'*Drunken* loud-mouth,' I waved my glass in the air, spilling it right across everybody's plates. 'Get it right, bumtongue, before you start calling me names. Better people have been there before!'

A loud cheer supported my outcry, not just from my table, but from surrounding ones eager to join in our fun.

'Not the sort of stuffed shirts I want to encourage in here, anyway,' sniffed the proprietor in the direction of their departing backs. 'Rather have life-lovers like you and your lot, Eve. Spend more for a start.'

He was right there. I paid for the treat. My television fee up the spout before it had even hit my hand. I resolved on a

43

life of restraint if I was to start saving.

They poured me onto the sleeper. I dropped my portable typewriter onto the platform as I was trying to climb up into the train. From the crash I could tell that I might as well leave it there.

'S'only a cheap one,' I smiled at the night steward, who was gallantly attempting to aid me aboard as my friends pushed from behind. But my foothold was feeble, I missed the final step and fell back against the flailing arms. We collapsed, all of us, screaming with helpless laughter back on the platform again. All in a heap on the ground.

'Jeesus . . . I'm pissin' m'self . . . can't stop,' a girl's voice screamed in the midst of us. More peals of laughter. I was in danger of doing the same, wetting myself. There'd been no time for the lavatory in the rush to catch the train. Not when we'd had to down our third Gaelic coffee.

'Dear God in heaven, come to my aid!' The steward stepped down and yanked me to my feet, half carrying me onto the train. Just in time for the train and its departure. But not for me and the lavatory. By the time I scrambled there I was already trickling all along the corridor, so I sat down on the open seat and piddled happily straight through my peach satin, lace trimmed, Janet Reger pants. And when I locked my compartment behind me I threw them, dripping, out through the window. Someone outside Taunton was going to get lucky. A fifteen quid pair of luxury knickers, in perfect condition, apart from a soaking crotch. And all they needed was a quick swill under the hot tap. 'Now why didn't I do that then, 'stead of chuckin' 'em away?' I addressed myself in the mirror. And I tottered over to the open window again and proffered outspread fingers to the night wind, on the offchance that whoever had found them, may already at this moment be flinging them back at me, in disgust. 'No such fuckin' luck, darlin',' I addressed the mirror again. 'Bloody silly train goin' the opposite direction!'

The discreet tap on the door heralded the arrival of the steward.

'Anything madame requires for the moment? Tea?' His eyes flickered over my damp inner thighs as I sprawled back on the bunk. My skirt had risen high enough for him to glimpse the darkness of my wet pubic hair. But I was past caring. I spread my legs wider, but with more grace – well, as much as I could muster.

'Whisky. Li'l'ole whisky?' I measured it with my fingers, screwing my eyes up to further emphasise the smallness of the drop that I required. 'Tiny, Y'understan', teeny-weeny, a bitty-bitty-boo? Oh, an' cup tea be lovely . . .'

I felt great, just GREAT! Going back to the big city, completely arse holed and incontinent, complained about by fellow-diners, an easy lay on British Railway, my knickers whirling amongst the stars, a cup of tea on its way, accompanied by the biggest whisky that a bucket could hold : . .

Who needed a fuckin' husband to tell me how to behave! Every other woman in the world, sure . . . but suck on it, sisters . . . I've bitten those balls . . . twice . . . hiccup . . .jus' havin' a li'l' puke in this pillow . . .

'Eve, darling, you look like a gorilla's armpit. I repeat, like a GORILLA'S ARMPIT!'

'Just cut the crap, Clifford, and get me a cup of coffee. I promise I'll make you the chief beneficiary.'

'What's that mean, Eve?'

'It means, Clifford, my angel, that when I die – like in the next five minutes, here in your kitchen – you're going to be left everything in my will. If I get the black coffee. Capito?

'Capito, eh? Speaka da Spanish? Did I ever tell you, Eve, darling about the . . .'

'Cliff!'

'Coffee on its way, Eve.'

'Another, please. And when I've drained that, keep on pouring. Cliff, I love you. Will you marry me?'

'Eve. It's Tuesday morning. You're at the Chelsea Arts Club. You've just got off the sleeper from Devon. It's not even eight in the morning yet. But you are very drunk indeed.'

'Still drunk from last night, Clifford. Don't tell me that it's never happened to you, you moralising fart. It's not what I need, a sermon. I've finished with all that.'

'I know, darling. He left your rooms yesterday.'

'I should hope he has. That was the arrangement, he's gone to stay with friends.'

'Word is that he may go back to America, darling.'

I lifted my head with immense difficulty. 'You know more than me then, Clifford.'

'Only a rumour. You know what this club's like. Every one knows every one's business. I stay outside it, myself. He's left you a sweet little note though. It's on the table by the bed, you can't miss it. Beautifully written, very loving. If you ask me, you two'll be back together in no time. I know a perfect match when I see it.'

'You've read the note, then? My private property. Bit of a nerve, Clifford.'

'Couldn't resist. I've taken over the cleaning of the bed-rooms now, an extension of duties. Bit of extra cash, I can do with it too, I can tell you. All right for you, Eve. Money you're making. Doing a telly with Diana Dors today, aren't you? I know, I met one of the sound technicians from Southern TV the other night in the Coleherne. He told me. Christ – you look BAD! You all right, darling? Best get back into bed for a couple of hours' proper kip. Never get a proper night's rest on those bloody sleepers. I'll bring you up a cup of tea later, when I've finished the breakfasts. Right load of berks staying here at the moment. Ugliest bunch of buggers this side of Bridlington!'

I went straight to bed, as Clifford advised. And didn't even wake up to drink his cup of tea, it was there, cold by my bed when consciousness finally dawned at around two in the afternoon. I'd had to get a move on then. Sort out what exotica I'd wear for the telly thing, have a bath, wash my hair (I'd had the roots re-tinted before I'd left Devon), and then order a cab to take me to Waterloo Station. We were pre-recording the show at Southern Television in Southampton.

Nail-biting time, awaiting the arrival of the taxi. Some traffic delay, they told me when I rang the firm. But after twenty minutes, I couldn't bear the tension any longer, so just hailed a passing cab. I got to Waterloo with just five minutes to spare. Nausea enveloped me when I shut my eyes to try and sleep. I cursed last night's celebration, and the second and third Gaelic coffee. But thanked Christ that at least the steward's whisky hadn't materialised. He'd apologised in the morning but excused himself on the grounds that he was looking after my best interests. I gave him an extra large tip with the morning pot of tea. I felt that he'd behaved like a decent human being. And I could tell that he hadn't taken advantage of my body either, because I awoke in exactly the same position as I'd fallen asleep. Fully clothed (minus my drawers), with the stench of vomit stinging my nostrils. Very edifying, very dignified indeed.

The make-up girls in the Southern studios were geniuses. I remembered them from other shows I'd done there. They needed to be today.

'Piss-holes in the snow, I'm afraid.' I pointed to my eyes. 'I leave it to you to work miracles.'

'With that hat on your head, who'll be looking at your face anyway! Fabulous, isn't it!'

'A David Shilling,' I said. 'One of the first he ever made me, but still a favourite of mine.'

'You've lost a lot of weight, haven't you, Eve?' The head of make-up walked into the room. 'Mind, I haven't seen you for over a year, you've been living in America, haven't you? All diet-conscious, aren't they over there. What did they do, get you jogging through Central Park before breakfast?' We both laughed.

'Not me, no bloody fear. I don't go in for jogging. You can lose your ankles that way. The bones get ground down onto the feet. Happened to a pal of mine. And I can't afford to lose any length from my legs. I'm a pit-pony from Wales, we value our inches. Nothing of the race-horse about me.'

I liked it in the make-up rooms of television studios. It was almost the most enjoyable part of doing a show. Someone sculpting a glamour mask on, while you just lie back and let it happen. Like being a woman of wealth, spending hours being manicured, and face-masked, and generally pampered. I could take to that sort of life if I found the right man. A millionaire with a liking for drunken loud-mouths.

Trouble was that I had never, ever, been drawn to men with money. I didn't get on well with materialists, which is what men with millions have to be. Whether they've made it themselves or inherited their wealth, it's still their greatest preoccupation. I'd had a ravishing girlfriend who'd become a British starlet in the flourishing film industry here in the fifties, at about the same time as Diana was our leading sex-symbol. And this girl, after making a love-marriage with an art teacher with whom she'd been a student, then splitting up with him, married a chap with millions. He even part-owned his own bank. But once when I was around there to dinner, he didn't utter a word throughout the entire meal.

'Anything the matter?' I'd whispered. 'Have you two had a tiff?'

'No, nothing like that. He just goes into these moods when he's worried about money. He's grumbling that we're down to our last four million.'

She'd had an affair with Sammy Davis, Junior, I remembered now. She used to boast about it to her husband's jealous fury.

'One-eyed, nigger-yid, runt!' That's what the husband called him, which struck me as racialist even then, when the word racialist hadn't become an accepted word in everyone's vocabulary. And odd, too, since he himself was Jewish and wore thick-lensed spectacles for his short sight. Plain people are usually the most critical of other people's physical attributes. The beauties rarely throw stones.

But perhaps, I'd been thinking lately, a millionaire was just what I could do with. Just to ease my mind a little over money matters. It didn't need to be a Rockefeller, or a Getty or a Howard Hughes. I'd settle for a moderate millionaire, someone on a smaller scale. Spring and Scarlett had agreed with me, when I'd brought up the subject on the phone after the American Express business. But then Scarlett, who tends to be a little more realistic than Spring, pointed out that I might find them incompatable to live with. And in any case, she'd also pointed out that to be a millionaire you'd have to be into possessions. Possessions of the finest kind, like the best works of art, or the fastest cars, or the grandest houses, or – she'd paused, weighing her words carefully, taking care to present her case with the maximum of tact, not to upset me, I supposed – or the most beautiful women, the *youngest*, most beautiful women.

So that let me out. I understood what she meant. And, indeed, agreed with her absolutely. Yes, millionaires were shit. But then hadn't I always said so. That wasn't going to be the way to solve my financial future.

The David Shilling hat was already giving me a headache, my hangover was just beginning to thump in true earnest. I would most certainly have to have a drink before I went in front of the cameras. But I'd done so much television by now that I had got it down to a fine art. How much to imbibe before actually going onto a show, especially a chat show like this one, where the aim was to sparkle.

I'd been introduced to my fellow guests, they were here in make-up at the moment, with me, being given their final powdering. One was a male stripper, a handsome, cheeky-eyed chap. Scarlett would have described him as 'hunky', something to get hold of. The other was a dotty grande dame, eccentric and outspoken, an aristocrat, a Lady, the sort that Britain produces best. She would have been a wow in the States. When we used to turn on the television over there it seemed that on every single chat show we'd see zany Hermione Gingold fluting away in her inimitable, croaky contralto. English to the tip of her chrysanthemum, crazy, hairstyle. Embarking upon anecdote after anecdote, sheer flights of her own fancy. The audience just couldn't get enough of her.

'That's it then is it,' this one chortled now, peering at herself in the mirror of the make-up room. 'Spot of paint on the old battleship – all ready for inspection!'

Then she turned to me. 'This old girl's gasping for a stiff scotch and soda, m'dear. Don't know about you!'

'I'll join you,' I countered eagerly.

The male stripper seemed in not the same sort of hurry as us.

'The lad's probably wise to steer clear of alcohol. Detrimental effect on the male equipment, y'know, alcohol. Could prove disastrous in his professional calling, wouldn't you say?'

She confided this to me along the corridor to the hospitality room. I had to break into a run to keep up with her stride. But her whisky and soda were beckoning. The confidence was imparted in a husky boom, the sort that would have struck terror to a whole battalion of troops. The male stripper, still in make-up, would most certainly have heard.

'As a patriot, m'dear, in the wartime,' she continued as we rounded a corner, 'I drove an ambulance. Certainly opened my eyes in the officers' mess. Lily-livered, the whole lot of 'em. Couldn't hold their liquor. I'd drink them under the table. Praise the Lord, we've arrived! Follow me – age before beauty!'

I trailed in behind her, enthralled, rendered speechless. She made a spectacular entrance, flinging the door wide.

'We've made it!' She announced, and drew me to her side, holding my hand in the air as if she was the referee and I'd just won the fight. 'Splendid, isn't she, gentlemen?'

The entire room turned from the television set, which they'd been watching in spellbound silence to stare at me.

'Extraordinary,' someone murmured. Then they turned back to the set again. I peered to see what they were watching. It was Diana down on the studio floor, surrounded by technicians adjusting the lighting of the set which had been designed to look like a luxurious living room. The sort a film star would have. Now she was crossing to a white piano, where a black pianist was seated. The sound men were testing the pitch as she broke into song. She was working hard, being professional, but had still to go to make-up and get changed.

'Hm, going to be here some time by the looks of things. Always command you to come too early. Terrified that one won't turn up at all, or not until the last mo. Better get stuck into the booze, what do you say!'

No-one was taking any notice of us, but at that moment the door burst open. It was the producer, his research assistant, and a young girl who could have doubled for Alice-in-Wonderland.

'Granny!' The girl rushed forward. 'We've been looking all over for you!'

'We thought you'd got lost.' The producer stretched out

his hand. 'Welcome to the show.'

'What will you have to drink?' The researcher moved through the room, returning with glasses and one of the opened bottles of white wine, which was the only thing on offer. My fellow guest inspected the label.

'Hm, I see. Gut-rot, count me out. I'll settle for a Scotch and soda. A *large* one,' she added firmly, then turned to me.

'Oh, well . . . well . . .' I needed spirits too, but understood the complications. The white wine wasn't there simply for economy reasons, but to ensure that whoever was appearing on the show wouldn't become too incapable before it started. Looking around the rest of the room, I recognised several other famous faces. Diana was taping more than one show tonight in front of a live studio audience. These others were obviously her guests too, though were not appearing with my new pal and me. They had glasses of wine in their hands, had resigned themselves to it, however undrinkable. To do otherwise now might create a situation of some awkwardness. But my pal was expecting moral support. I had allied myself with her.

'I'll have a gin and tonic,' I added bravely, 'with ice and lemon. Large too, please.'

The researcher looked nervously at the producer.

'Means going down to the bar . . .'

'Splendid, then, that's settled. Oh, what will you have, darling Fiona? A small sherry, yes. A small sherry, please, for my granddaughter, if you'd be so kind.'

The producer nodded helplessly at the researcher, who scuttled away. 'Let me explain about the show, folks . . .' He was addressing the whole room now, including us. My new pal winked at me, and I laughed back at her. Our particular show was already a pre-determined success.

Diana was beaming at us. The studio audience was clapping and clapping. The credits were rolling and the fade-out music was playing. The show was over, we could sit back and relax.

'That was *sensational, * darlings! *Really sensational!*' Diana sat, shimmering from head to foot in turquoise sequins, exuding a womanly sexuality. Full-breasted, soft-fleshed, a

51

larger than life vision of platinum and peach with a pussy-cat smile. Warm as toast. And the easiest, most relaxed interviewer that I'd yet had.

'To sum up,' she'd concluded it all by saying, 'what would you both consider the qualities of the ideal man, ladies?' My pal answered first.

'Kindness. Generosity. Intelligence. Humour. Good looks. But undoubtedly, most important of all, the size of his equipment.'

When the programme went out, some months later in the spring, I watched. Not to see myself, I was never interested in myself on the screen, but to see whether they had kept that best bit of her answer in. They hadn't. But when she'd said it, this eighty-year-old, all the women in the audience had cheered. Most of them were themselves well past middle age. I thought it was very revealing, how mulish the reaction was from their men.

We'd shared a studio car back to London, this splendid creature and myself. Alice-in-Wonderland slept all the way.

'She's very lucky,' I looked at the child, she couldn't have been more than sixteen. 'She has a wonderful grand-mother.' We smiled at each other, there had been instant rapport from the start.

'I have other grandchildren, older. And great-grandchildren too, all as enchanting. I lose count how many, though they come and see me all the time. Families are important to a woman. Families and lovers, I've always believed that. I had a very nice husband, we were the best of friends. But I didn't meet the love of my life until I was fifty and my children were grown-up. We were to get married. I was going to leave my husband and he was going to leave his wife. But he got killed in the war. So I stayed with Bertie, of course there were other men . . . but in my heart there has only ever been that one.'

I held her hand all the way back to London.

Six

'I've got a black eye . . . I'm all bruised. I'm leaving him . . .
can I sleep with you tonight . . .' Spring was sobbing on the
phone.

'My baby, what happened?' I was appalled by the *terrible*
sound of her. Clifford was lurking around the telephone
booth down in the hall, pretending to dust the letter-rack.
Trying to listen in. I raised two fingers, as a fuck-off sign, in
his direction. He grinned good-naturedly – it was well-nigh
impossible for me to offend Clifford. But he took the hint
and went through into the cocktail bar. I turned around,
giving my undivided attention now to my distraught
daughter.

'We had a terrible fight again . . . we keep having them
lately. He did this to me a couple of months ago . . . beat me
up really badly . . . I couldn't go to work . . . and when I
did the bruises were still there all over my face. And, and
. . . David, who was directing the play I was on then . . . he
and some of the actors said they'd go and beat Joe up . . .
they were all shocked, I looked so . . .' She choked, unable
to continue. And then she went on. I could feel the cold
fury, even in my teeth, that someone had done this to my
child. *I'd kill him.*

'Anyway, they made me promise that if he ever did it
again that I'd leave him . . . and I said to him last night that
if he hit me I'd go . . . but he hit me anyway . . . and left me
lying on the floor in the flat and he slammed the door and
went out . . . and didn't come back, thank . . . thank good-
ness. But I was frightened that he would come back and
start all over again, kicking me. So I bolted the door and I
. . . I started ringing you. But you weren't there, Mum.
Mum, where were you . . . I needed you . . . I wanted to
come to you . . .'

Her wailing whipped at my conscience. Why hadn't I been there when she'd needed me. But how could I have known – I'd thought she and Joe were so happy together, consumed only with my own shattering situation. My selfishness blinding me to the possibility of anyone else's problems.

'Little one,' I soothed, 'I'm so sorry I wasn't here. I didn't get back from Southampton until after midnight. I came in the studio car, it was too late for the train. You remember I told you I was doing the television thing.' The sobbing was subsiding, but the catch in the voice was still there.

'I forgot. I forgot about the television. I thought that you'd gone out . . . out with Adam . . . and that you wouldn't be coming back . . . and I wouldn't know how to find you . . . I just needed to hear your voice . . . Mum.'

'My darling baby – I'm here now. I would have been here if I hadn't been working. You know that I'd never have been out with Adam, you know that. It's over, baby, you've helped me over it.' The sobbing, softer now, started again.

'It's over with Joe too. Oh, Mum, tell me, just tell me what I'm going to do. I've got nowhere to go to. I've got nowhere to live. I'll have to go back to sharing with girls again, or get a terrible bed-sit. We've been together nearly two years, I can't live on my own now. I'd *hate* it. I'll get fat, I'll start eating chocolate again. I'll look horrible and nobody'll want me . . .'

'That'll be the day, Spring. Don't make me laugh.' And I laughed anyway. 'I didn't notice much shortage, even when you went up to – what was it, eleven stone?'

'I was twelve stone by the end. When you went to live down in Devon, before you left for the States.' A mournful voice but more normal. The crying had ceased.

'Were you really? Well, you were still gorgeous. What are you now?'

'Just under eight, but I'm not eating, hardly anything. Just smoking a lot. Joe hates me fat.'

'Just under eight stone. Not enough, not for your height. You could do with putting on a bit. I think you've overdone this bloody diet lark now. Anyway, who gives a sod what Joe thinks. You're leaving him – remember? Tonight you move in with me, you sleep here in the little room. I'll get a heater put in. And then I'll work out some place to live, you leave it all to me. Nothing to worry about, nothing at all, not any more. You've got your mother, remember that. Old Mumples is here.'

I put down the phone after she'd gone and stood there, thinking, just thinking.

'Problems, Eve, darling? Anything I can do to help?' Clifford's concerned face appeared at my shoulder. 'These just don't seem to be your times, do they? I wonder what your horoscope for today says, whether there are going to be any more disasters in store. I've got last night's *Evening Standard* out in the kitchen. I set great store by that Patric Walker, he's always right about me. Last Wednesday he said for me to watch out for friendships which might lead to disappointment. And do you know he was right. That very evening in the Markham Arms I'd been certain of at least two tricks. I was just playing one off against the other. And guess what happened – the tarts went off with each other, great looking fellas, both of them. Oh, I stamped my tiny foot then, you can imagine! Do you want me to get it for you? What sign are you anyway? Let me guess, darling – I guess, um, I guess Aquarius. Right?'

'Right!' I whirled around, filled with a sudden resolve. 'Yes, Cliff, let's have a look at your paper. They have flats to let in the *Standard*, don't they. Cross fingers, I could be out of here by the end of the week. I could be installed in a cosy home, a nice nest for me and my daughter, never mind where it is. All she needs now, at this moment, is a sense of security.' I smiled triumphantly at Clifford. His stricken face stared back.

'You're never leaving the club, Eve? I thought you were a permanent fixture. What's going to happen to me? I'll have no-one to talk to again. It'll be like it was before you came . . .'

I felt sorry for Clifford, I knew just how he felt. There were a lot of snotballs in the club who merely regarded him as a toast-singeing, bacon-burning, tea-brewing machine. A bit of a temperamental oddity. I gave him a hug, a proper hug, so that he knew how I felt about him.

'We won't lose sight of each other, Cliff. We're good friends, you and I. By the way, I think you probably had a lucky escape with those two tarts in the Markham. Those good-looking guys always get all the action, never stop. They would probably have given you a social disease.'

'Wrong there, Eve. I'd have given it to them.'

'Great! I'll give breakfast a miss 'til you're cured. Just keep taking the pills – see you later.'

I filled the bath with hot water and poured Badedas into it, thinking of the Badedas ads. *Anything can happen after a Badedas bath.* That's what the captions read, beneath the photo of a female nude, draped in a towel, just round the bottom of her bum. With a passionate Latin outside smouldering up at her bathroom window. Blimey, mind-boggling stuff! I peered out of my own window on the offchance of a stray serenader. Not a single sod in sight, only the ageing road-sweeper, who'd been doing this street for the past sixteen years. So much for advertisements – though, I reminded myself, this was still before and not after. Still a chance when I stepped out for anything to happen. I might have found the ideal flat in the *Standard*, for instance.

I settled back in the steamy luxury to study the Property Column, turning from Homes For Sale, through to Flats and Maisonettes To Let, ending up at Board, Residence and Apartments. Nothing! A big, fat blank! So much, I thought again, for bloody Badedas. I could sue them on the Trades Description Act, leading a person on to high hopes and then not coming up with the goods.

I was appalled by the price of accommodation, but then it was six years since I'd last lived in London. There was no comparison between Devon, or even New York, and here. If I were to get anything at all decent I was going to have to fork out the earth, and though I'd always felt confident that I could capture the entire universe whenever I wished, mere earth was not quite at my disposal at this moment in time. I didn't own a single tree of it, not a shrub, nor even a weed. I spiralled down into depression. Then I let more water into the bath from the hot tap, turned on the tiny transistor radio and slumped down beneath the bubbles to enjoy wallowing in my own misery.

'And now for our Golden Oldie!' The hysterical jargon of the manic disc-jockey on Capital Radio. 'Back to the Swinging Sixties with the one and only . . . Rolling Stones! Remember this one, folks? I CAN'T GET NO SATISFACTION . . .'

The record took me right back, back to the summer of '64. The summer I spent in Marbella.

I'd had two invitations to holiday in the sun that summer, both from supposed millionaires. I chose the wrong one, of course, the confidence trickster. A gambling pal of Lord Lucan (where *was* Lord Lucan now?), who'd lost his inheritance at casinos all over the world. The other, a film-maker, had gone on to amass further millions by making documentaries on the Duke of Windsor and Winston Churchill, both with much footage of exclusive in-depth interviews. But that one, the film-maker, didn't like children and I had no intention of leaving Spring and Scarlett behind. So I went to Marbella, to a villa on the shore, and found to my surprise (and relief) that my host had his Swedish mistress installed. Far from being expected to pay for the holiday with sexual favours, I was led to understand after the first week that straight cash was preferred. It was termed as a loan, for my host had run out of pesetas (temporarily embarrassed, darling). The amount suggested was staggering. He must have thought that I was living on a colossal alimony from Henry, for Henry always gave the impression of being immensely wealthy. It was clear to me that after paying it I'd have to cut the holiday short and fly back that very weekend. The kids had enjoyed the sea and sand, were thoroughly pampered by the entire houseparty. Sophisticates, unused to adorable moppets. But there were no flights available, I'd had to wait a few days before the arranged departures. That's when I met the young playboy. The day intended for my departure came and went – I was neck-high in a holiday romance.

I never completely understood how I caught him. Until we were introduced, he had been squiring the Swedish girlfriend of my host's mistress. She was staying with him in another villa a short way along the coast. And faced with the bikini-ed and sensational shapeliness of this flaxen-haired, pouty-mouthed, Scandinavian siren compared to me in my modest one-piece (concealing the ravaged belly resulting from childbirth), I knew without hesitation who I would have chosen.

But I made him laugh, so he said. And he found me sexy, he didn't know why. But all he could think about, from the very second he set eyes on me, was SEX. I oozed with the stuff, he'd never been so instantly turned on like that by any bird before in his whole life, never fancied a chick – *really* fancied, so that he wanted to fuck there on the dance-floor – that had never happened before . . . Jesus, I was just what he'd been looking for . . .

Which was very important, very important indeed. The dashing young playboy was impotent.

We met at the Marbella Club. I'd gone with my suave host, the confidence trickster, having difficulty in hooding the hatred I now harboured towards him for having duped me. Me, bright as a button usually when it came to sussing out character. It wasn't the money I'd minded, it was the being taken for a fool. And I'd forced myself to give a (free) fuck to this toad too, though he wasn't at all my type, as a show of gratitude when he'd invited me and the children to stay in his holiday villa. I'd have been better off going to Brighton, instead of struggling to keep up with these international jet-setters. Completely out of my depth. Admired only because of my amusingly original appearance (a superannuated art student), my ready supply of raunchy expletives and the valued ability to return a politically offensive remark with an entertainingly outrageous insult. They *loved* that, all this crowd. The way I derided them and their dilettante attitude to everything in life.

Up until that time I'd been an artist, a proper one, not a Sunday painter. I'd spent five years at art college. I'd taught art in a school. I'd appeared in a prestigious underground movie (fully clothed). I'd opened my own boutique after making the hats and bags for Biba Boutique, which had been the first to open in London's swinging sixties. I'd run my own restaurant (though only for six weeks, at the end of which time I simply put SHUT on the door – not even bothering to do the washing up), cleverly managing to enlarge my liver to twice what it had been before, lapping up liqueurs pressed upon me by contented customers. The enlarged liver was one of my major achievements, a valued future contribution to medical research. I'd been offered and had accepted the much sought-after position as Fashion Editor of a recently published glossy magazine, revolutionary in its attitude to women's role in the society of the day. I had married a man and divorced him, scorning his financial support now that I had the magazine job to go back to at the end of this holiday.

But finally, I had given birth to two other human beings. My greatest achievement. Which meant more than any of the other paltry activities put together.

And what had they done, these lotus-eaters? Bugger all, except chase the sun throughout the year. Snow- and ski-bound in winter. Sea- and sand-blown in summer. Except they even lacked the imaginative energy to adapt themselves to their environment.

I was the only one who spent the day on the beach. Building sandcastles with Spring and Scarlett, swimming in the sea with them, eating lunchtime sardines in the shade of the beach café, snoozing off the effects of the wine (water with theirs, half and half, in the continental manner), then telling them stories as the sun finally dipped. Each of them cuddling up to me, one on either side, all three of us snug and warm in our ritzy towelling robes (half-price in the Harrods sale, bought to show off on the beach). And it was never until then that our fellow house-guests ever joined us.

They spent the day sleeping! I couldn't get over it, in the same way that they couldn't understand where I found the energy to dance until dawn with them and not spend the same amount of time as them in bed. But they didn't have children. Mine, more often than not, would be starting to wake up by six or seven in the morning, which was when we'd usually return from our clubbing. The most that Spring and Scarlett would allow me was a couple of hours in bed. They would lie quietly with their books and toys for only so long, then they'd struggle into their miniscule swimsuits. Sugar-candy striped they were that year. Then they'd come with beach towels in their small hands and stand silently, close to my sleeping face, just staring down It would have been inhuman to ignore the appeal.

But all that changed when I met the playboy. We moved into his villa, which had its own private beach with Spanish servants who doted on the English bambinos. They could run out of their beds as early as they liked, they didn't need me to keep an eye on them in the shallows of the sea. Or even to help build their sandcastles, the Spanish maids did it better. So gradually a new holiday pattern emerged. My suntan suffered because I spent the mornings in bed now but by then I really needed the rest. My playboy's impotence was proving pretty exhausting . . .

I CAN'T GET NO SATISFACTION. That had been the record at the Marbella Club that summer. It summed up that sexual relationship, because for me – apart from the ultimate tedium of trying to tongue life into that timid tadpole – I was finding it pretty damn frustrating. A full four weeks without a fuck. No wonder I was insatiable when I got back to London, it was a case of making up for lost time!

The record was coming to an end, listening to the potent virility of the young voice, the Jagger magic, I thought of the last time that I'd met Mick. It was in New York, not long before Adam and I had left. My pal, Anita Pallenberg, had taken us to the party which was being thrown in a Manhattan disco to launch the latest Stones album. He looked good, athletic and healthy, amongst all that crowd. Time seemed not to have touched him at all. Jerry Hall was seeing to his every need, going up to the bar to get the drinks and paying for them like everybody else. It surprised me to see her counting the change from her dollar bills, but then I never bother to check my change (which was why Jerry has cash in the bank and I haven't).

Keith Richards joined us, greeting Anita affectionately although they were no longer together. But they'd had two cildren together, there would always be a link.

'Champagne, Eve?' Anita's warmth embraced everybody. But she and I escaped to the bar before the force of the tones' fans threatened to separate us. We toasted each other.

I'll miss you, kid, when I go back.' I squeezed her satin-lad shoulder. She lifted her glass.

'Same here. Where are you going to be living? Don't orget to give me your address.'

'Well, there is no address yet. God only knows where we'll live – have you got any ideas? We're like fucking gypsies roaming the earth.'

'There's always the house in Cheyne Walk. That's been empty for years, it was burgled three times in twelve months. Isn't that terrible! Just because nobody's in it.' She'd shrugged. 'It's there if you want it, I'll just have to check with Keith, but I'm sure it'll be all right. Only thing is . . I don't think you'll much like it . . .' She hadn't elaborated beyond that, instead had given me the number of the Rolling Stones' office in London with the name to the person to talk to should I decide to take up her offer.

I had forgotten all about it. Until now.

Seven

'It's a big old bugger, isn't it!' I stood at the wrought-iron garden gate, still outside on the pavement of Cheyne Walk. Just contemplating the heating costs alone of this house. Neville, from the Stones' office, chuckled and clanged his bunch of keys. When we mounted the steps and reached the solid front door, he selected several from the bunch and inserted them in various keyholes.

'Big enough for one, I should have thought. Six floors, fifteen rooms, four bathrooms. You'll be rattling around having a great time, you and the ghosts!'

I shivered. It was a fine day, the sun was shining and there was still warmth in it although we were now in October. But, standing there on the doorstep, I was suddenly chilled to the marrow. Icy cold.

'Oh, I'll be sharing the premises? That'll be fun.' I forced a laugh. The front door swung open onto the completely dark corridor of the hallway. The only daylight filtering through to it came from a casement window on the first landing of the far staircase.

'Only joking. Hey, you hold on there a minute while organise some light.' I was left on my own whilst Neville disappeared into a room to the right of the corridor. turned my back and stared deliberately through the open front door to the street outside. The sunny normality of the scene somehow reassured me.

'All fixed!' I turned around. Above my head swung a naked bulb, low wattage. I'd have to get a brighter one there if I was going to live here. I'd always believed in a welcoming glow the moment I entered anywhere. Even so far as to having those doormats, the height of kitsch, with WELCOME printed on them. At this moment, all this house was saying was GO AWAY. SOD OFF!

'That's great! You're a clever lad, Neville!' I said it admiringly.

'No great knack. It's just that these lights have a mind of their own. You'll find that out, but it's nothing to be scared of. I'll show you how to twiddle the switches. Now, shall we start with the basement and just work our way to the top?' He led the way down a narrow flight of stairs, wooden, with no carpet, and then selected a different key from the bunch again.

'Shouldn't think you'll be venturing down here very often. Unless you want to adjust the heating. The boiler's down here, runs on oil.'

'I must say it's very warm in the house. Is it as warm as this all the way up? It delighted me, the high temperature of the house, used as I had become to the torrid central heating in the Eden Apartments, where we had lived in New York. The Chelsea Arts Club hadn't progressed with the times, their rooms were heated by inadequate single-bar electric fires. Already I'd been dreading a cold spell, a change for the worse in the weather. I feel the cold more than most, for some reason. Irrationally, Adam always claimed.

'All the way, every nook and cranny. Has to be kept dry, this house, being so close to the Thames. All these buildings along the Embankment would deteriorate in no time if the damp was allowed to take over. We keep the heat on all through the year. Regardless of whether anyone is here or not.'

I felt relieved by his words. That's all that had been worrying me, the cost of the heating. So it was their responsibility, not mine, if I moved in.

The basement consisted of four rooms, obviously designed to be servants' quarters in their time. *Upstairs, downstairs.* That syndrome of social demarcation. Despite the heat from the boiler-room, it was dank. It smelt of death. Again I was growing icily cold. I drew my coat more closely around me, but I couldn't control an involuntary shudder and found myself moving closer to Neville. As close as I could to this kid without it looking like some sort of pass. I coughed and cleared my throat.

'Spooky down here, isn't it?' He nodded his head without smiling. Though he was a smiling person.

'Sure is.' Then he turned to go back up the stairs to the hallway, saying over his shoulder. 'Are you really going to be staying in the house on your own? If so, rather you than me. I couldn't spend a single night here, I can tell you.'

'My daughter is meant to be staying with me, for a while anyway.' I'd said 'meant to be' because just before I'd left the club this afternoon to come and see this morgue, Spring had rung up.

She'd sounded radiant this time.

'We've had a long talk about things, Joe and I. And we're going to dinner tonight after I finish at the theatre to try to sort ourselves out. I *may* come on to stay with you, but then again I may not. Is that all right, Mum?'

'Absolutely all right, my precious. You do what you think best. There's always someone up late at the club to let you in.' So that was that, I thought. It isn't so easy to leave someone after all. Didn't I know that! And though their affair may be grinding to a painful halt, this dinner was to be a reconciliation, however small. Spring would spend tonight with Joe, and would stay with him too. For a while. Whether it was a week, or a month, who could tell? Either way I had to prepare and feather a nest for her to fall into, I felt that I owed her that as a friend. And mother.

The light flickered on the basement stairs as we climbed back to the hallway. Though Neville had re-locked the door behind us, the one which led through to the basement rooms, I had an uncanny sensation that it was still open. And that . . . I was . . . being watched. By more than one person.

'You see what I mean.'

'What!' My voice was high with rising hysteria. I couldn't wait to leave these stairs behind – and whatever else I may be leaving, lurking down there in the darkness.

'You see what I mean, about the lights.' As he said it, the flickering light bulb extinguished itself, taking exception to Neville's criticism. Spiting both of us for our intrusion, but me in particular. I tripped on the turn of the steps and fell up the last four. Winded, and shaken, not just from the fall but from the satisfied malevolence in the surrounding gloom. Stifling me.

'Are you OK?' Neville helped me to my feet. I dusted myself down, childishly close to tears. Get a hold of yourself, woman, I said to myself. Otherwise this nice kid is going to think you're a raving neurotic instead of the rational adult you are. But I'd always had a dread of darkness and the imagined unknown.

As a child I'd longed to sleep with the light on all night, but, my mother said we couldn't afford it. Waste of electricity. All we could run to was a candle, but, if anything, that was even more frightening than pitch-blackness. The flickering shadows, the ever-shifting shapes on the ceiling, the leaping ogres across the wall. I'd had to shut them out with my eyelids, but still they'd remain printed on my retina. So that my dreams were invaded regularly by nightmares, such that I'd do anything to put off the evil hour of my bedtime. I never told anyone why. I'd suffered too many scoldings from teachers at school for exaggeration of the facts, for ludicrous embroidery of the truth, for indulging in fantasy – for harbouring an over-active imagination. One of the reasons I was always accused of lying.

'This is the dining room.' Neville brandished one arm, the one with the keys. Even their jangling was jarring my nerves.

'I see,' I said looking round. All that the room contained was a long, dark, wooden refectory table and an ill-assorted scattering of high-backed kitchen chairs. Other than that there was a plastic coffee table at the far end of the room, by the front window. That too was surrounded by chairs, of a lounging nature. Easy chairs, representing the change in fashion over the past fifteen years. These were relics of the sixties. A modern pine rocker, its seat upholstered in a William Morris print. A vast Scandinavian cube, lacquered white, with expensive, toffee-coloured cushions in soft leather lining the inside. To sit in it would be to lose yourself forever in its sinking depths. I used to have one of those myself in the same era. I also had one of those whickerwork basket chairs hanging from the ceiling – a hateful thing in which you had to strain forward all evening just to be included in the conversation. When you sat back, nobody could see your face, nor could you hear what anyone was saying.

But they didn't have one of those here, though I had half expected it. Instead the gimmick was a set of airline seats, joined together, complete with a tilting device for reclining, and an ashtray in each of the armrests. Quite good fun, especially for kids. Spring and Scarlett would have adored it when they were young, taking it in turns to play the part of the air-hostess. Contriving to spill coffee on the other one's lap.

The rest were antiques, but I couldn't even begin to hazard a guess from which period they originated. Some looked Oriental to me, inlaid with milky mother-of-pearl. One must have been Egyptian. Another was clearly Indian, a temple piece, I should have said. But antiques have never interested me, I'd always found them faintly depressing. Steeped in history, my least favourite subject. Like this house, still lumbering in the past.

'It all looks rather – deserted.' I turned to follow Neville through into the kitchen.

'The burglaries,' he said, in a throw-away line, you see that – even the light-fittings were ripped from the walls. Well, this is the kitchen. Very little works in here actually. This old cooking range, all these vast ovens, they're absolutely useless. Outdated. But the little electric cooker, that works if you want to cook a meal. These sinks all have running water, hot when the heating's on. There's a big catering fridge out there in that little room.' He pointed out past the kitchen. My eyes followed his finger.

'Great! I'll be able to stack it up with champagne.'

'Good idea. You'll need something to give you Dutch courage. Right, onwards and upwards. I'm due back at the office in twenty minutes. When,' he asked over his shoulder,' were you thinking of moving in?'

'Well,' I must have sounded dubious.

'Mind you, I wouldn't blame you if you decided against it.'

'No,' I spoke quickly, I didn't have anywhere else to go.' It's nothing to do with the house. It just feels unlived in, that's all. I'll liven it up. I'll move in tomorrow, if it's all right with everyone. Tomorrow morning. I'll get my things brought over from the Chelsea Arts.'

'Fine. I'll leave you a set of these keys. Right, here we are. You won't be using this floor very much, I imagine!'

'I might want to go roller-skating, Neville.' I said it seriously, and we both laughed. The empty room, stained oak floor, solitary piano standing in the corner (covered with meticulously painted psychedelic patterns), this room extended from one end of the house to the other. The windows were fringed with the tassels of Eastern hangings, though behind them were black opaque roller blinds which would blot out any vestige of light were they pulled down. On the wall was a homage to the late Jimi Hendrix. And on the empty mantlepiece lay a framed photograph of Keith, with long hair and hippie clothes, gazing into some lighted candles.

Neville turned on one of the four switches by the door.

'See?' He pointed upwards to the ceiling. A big crystal ball began to rotate, scattering diamonds of light all over the room. For the first time I registered the chaise-longue against a far wall.

'Good for meditation, anyway.' The effect of the slow, silent circling and the emptiness of the room was mesmerising. I was prickling with uneasiness, terrified. But why I couldn't have said. After all it was only a common ballroom crystal ball. Hadn't I danced the last waltz, snuggling ecstatically to whoever had plucked me from the line of wallflowers for this final honour, hadn't I danced that, easily a hundred times beneath the same sort of ball. It had never unnerved me then, quite the opposite. I'd found it glamorous and dreadfully exciting. More than that – it had put me in the mood for anything on the walk home. In fact I'd sworn to myself that if I ever had the money, a crystal ball was what I'd really look forward to having in my own home. And here it was.

Why then was I finding it so macabre? Why did I feel it menacing me?

'I think that's the idea. Escape from the world. Not a soul could ever see a thing through those blinds. Safe as houses, as they say . . . It gets better from here up, this is where the bedrooms start. Oh, that's one of the bathrooms up there, but there's another one off this room. The master-bedroom.'

'A four-poster! Christ – it's magnificent!' I gasped at the opulence of the bed dominating the room. 'Jacobean, isn't it?'

Neville glanced at his watch. And he began moving from the bedroom back towards the staircase before I'd even had a chance to study the carved oak. *This was my room.* I had to sleep here. I'd fallen in love with the four-poster. I didn't care about seeing the rest of the house. I'd come to rest, the room sang to me. I could hear celestial choirs chorusing in my head. Every angel on the ceiling of the bed was smiling in my direction. The four winged figures bending from the four posters were beckoning me, they were my guardians. The carved foliage at the foot and head of the frame were opening their hearts and offering flowers . . .

'Time's running a bit short, I'm afraid. Do you want to look upstairs? They're all just bedrooms really, nothing special. Full of junk.' Neville was impatient to be back at the office.

'Oh, sorry, Neville. No, don't bother with the rest. I can look at them tomorrow when I come. Perhaps we'd better just sort out the keys. You must explain which one fits in where.'

After the explanation and the passing over of the keys, I strolled back to the club. On the way I bought a bottle of claret and some cheeses, an assortment. It didn't worry me that the old Aga ovens in the kitchen of Cheyne Walk didn't work. At one time it would have filled me with housewifely frustration. But not any longer, now that I no longer had a family to cook for. I'd given up eating meat after just one month in the States. I think that it was the gigantic servings of steak that put me off. Whatever, I no longer felt the need for a roast and two veg. That wasn't how I ate any more. I actually preferred snacking off cold food and wine. Alfresco style. I'd got used to a delicatessen diet.

But I bought a bottle of champagne as well. In case Spring hadn't managed to work it out with Joe. She might need a bubble of something, either in commisseration or celebration, the pop of the cork would lighten the occasion.

On the way I called into the Antique Market to say hello to Monika, who ran one of the jewellery stalls there. She was a nice girl. I liked her. Intriguing in an off-beat way, especially her accent. A strange mixture of Swiss-Cockney. People said we looked alike, but I couldn't see it. She was much younger than me, could have been my daughter, just about, at a pinch. And was tall, with the legs that I was meant to have, nearly as tall as Adam in fact. We'd both liked her, meeting her about two days after our arrival in London, with a mutual friend, gay.

'Do you think she'd be interested, that one?' Adam had asked me afterwards. I'd shrugged.

'Possibly. But it doesn't matter. She'd be just as nice as a friend, wouldn't she?' He snorted, in place of a proper reply.

Now she was startled to see me. I could tell that she was. Embarrassed, no doubt about the break-up, not quite knowing what to say. Whether to offer condolences or congratulations. I'd be getting a lot of that, now that I was back. This was the first confrontation with a friend though. I tried to put her at her ease when she asked me how I was. Her eyes could hardly meet mine, even before I answered. But she'd caught me at a good time.

'I'm great,' I said. 'I've found a wonderful place to live. I shall be moving out of the Chelsea Arts Club tomorrow morning and into the Stones' house on Cheyne Walk.' And I grinned, making sure to show every single molar in my mouth.

'Marvellous! I must come around for a cup of tea.'

'You must, Monika, once I've settled in.' I kept smiling at her, but an awkward silence had sprung up between us, so I said my goodbye and headed out towards the street. Her embarrassment stayed with me until I reached the club.

Clifford was scurrying through the hallway as I came through the door. I'd told him I was going to see the house.

'How was it, Eve? Horrible, I hope. So you're not leaving here after all.'

'Yes, I am leaving, Cliff. Tomorrow morning as a matter

of fact. It'll be my last breakfast tomorrow, you'd best make it a good one.'

'You don't eat them anyway. Getting to be a right bag-of-bones, you are. It's not flattering at your age to lose too much weight. You'll end up looking like the Duchess of Windsor. Raddled.'

I laughed, I understood his need to be spiteful. He'd miss me, but I'd miss him too and our light-hearted repartee. Who would I have to talk to in the mornings at Cheyne Walk? The oppressive silence of the house re-entered my thoughts, but I resolutely thrust it to one side.

'Come and have a drink with me here tonight, Cliff. That's if you've nothing better to do.' I spoke impulsively. 'Just a farewell tot. Be nice.'

'What – me have a drink here! You must be joking, darling – what would the members say?'

But he was coming anyway, I'd persuaded him. Sod the members.

Before his arrival was due I'd sorted through all my post. A horrifying bank statement which I viewed at arm's length without even putting on my glasses, so that the true figure was reassuringly blurred. A similarly alarming piece of correspondence from Access, showing I'd overspent my limit. The return of a massive restaurant bill with my accompanying cheque, which I'd neglected to sign. The monthly account from a small bookshop specialising in obscure examples of literary erotica – tomes which Adam chose to order on my behalf, but which only he read. To see if they were worthy of my attention. And an assortment of statements from various other places where we had accounts. All of them in debit.

I'd already started on the claret and taken a fresh gulp each time I'd opened yet another buff-coloured envelope. It had always deeply irritated both my husbands, what they termed to be my working-class preoccupation with money. The way I worried when I owed it. Henry, upper middle class, never minded being in debt. He always expected to be, never bothered to pay any bills until the threat of litigation was upon him. And Adam considered my concern to be simply *bourgeois*. A desire to ally myself with respectabil-

70

ity. Something he, as an artist, was above. Bully for him.

The claret was doing little to assuage my anxiety. I poured more, seeing to my surprise that now the bottle was nearly empty. Had I only purchased a half – or were they putting less in them these days! I turned to the rest of my correspondence, starting first with the telephone messages, masses of them which I'd collected from my pigeonhole downstairs. Many were from dear friends asking to see me, inviting me to dinner, wanting to have drinks. I opened my diary and made a note to ring two numbers from the pile.

Both were good girlfriends of mine, though they had also got on well with Adam. In fact it was through Adam that I'd met Patience. Patience and Jake, her present husband. Though I'd almost interviewed Jake Atkins when I was doing a newspaper piece on fringe performers and Jake was presenting his one-man show up at the Edinburgh Festival. He'd made it to the West End now, had an acclaimed show on at present. We'd been to see it, Adam and I, meeting up with Patience and Jake afterwards for dinner. Now I'd broken up our friendly foursome.

Tabitha Hunt was a pianist, a quirky pillar of this country's musical establishment although she'd been born and brought up in Boston. She'd come to London to study at the Royal College of Music and had fallen in love with and secretly married a brilliant but impoverished fellow student, from Yorkshire, on her eighteenth birthday. Her family didn't find out until two years later, by which time she'd become pregnant twice, each time miscarrying in the third month. She still had no children, though that first marriage had ended and she'd married again. This time she'd chosen the temperamental Welsh tenor, Rhys Williams. It had seemed ill-fated from the start, the union of two such charismatic individualists. And yet they remained together, in harmony, much longer than was expected. Over five years to be exact, and during that time their careers prospered. The fame of one serving to enhance that of the other, one of the celebrated married couples in the world of classical music. Until the press and public gradually grew to accept, indeed expect, that they would be together forever. It was at that point they separated, dramatically announced plans to divorce. Within a week of the decree absolute Rhys Williams married Tabitha's secretary.

'An insipid imitation of myself, darling, had I remained back in Boston with my ultra-conservative family. I'm the only hornet from that horrifying nest of wasps. But I think now that it was the discarded wasp in me that Rhys most admired. Thundering snobs, the Welsh working classes, aren't they.'

'Tabby, I'm Welsh and working class.'

'That's what I mean. You're one of the worst snobs, apart from my ex-husband, that I've ever met. You're an intellectual snob – I suppose that's forgivable. But it springs from the same source. You have such inferiority complexes. Probably comes from being so short. Now tell me, you know all about these things, what will I wear for tonight's recital.' She could charm the cherubs out of a church. But I'd been with her, comforting, when Rhys had absconded with half her heart. There wasn't much evidence of wit then, she'd wept in my arms.

'I want him back.' That's all she'd groaned, over and over again. And we'd got plastered together until both of us had passed out and I'd had to help sober her up again for a concert at the Festival Hall. The critics claimed that she'd rarely given such a brilliant performance.

I was getting plastered now, I must be because the bottle was empty. But I didn't feel it, not at all, just mellow and very relaxed. I looked at my watch, it was getting late. Clifford was meant to have been here almost an hour ago. I'd give him fifteen more minutes and then check to see if he wasn't waiting downstairs for me in the bar. In the meantime I'd better beautify myself.

I opened the wardrobe and looked at myself in the full-length mirror. It had an inaccuracy in it, this mirror, it gave you width and took away height. I'd turned in horror when I'd first seen my reflection and had vowed never to look at it again. And I hadn't, not until now. I'd always made use of the mirror in the corridor outside to check on what I was wearing. But now I was flabbergasted to see that the person

72

staring back at me was a different shape altogether from the one I was expecting. I'd shrunk. I was tiny, but in proportion to my width I was tall. Tall and skinny! I touched my tits to check that both balloons were still there, but even those constant companions (which never deserted me however much weight I lost) had tightened back on themselves. What I had now were two tennis balls as compared to a couple of buoys bouncing out at sea. And my bum – where was that? My seating equipment, so normally comfortable in chairs that I could survive a hard surface for hours without complaint, that was now through to the bone. Turning my head to one side, I noticed the lean neatness of jaw. The stretched flesh over my cheekbone was so tight that a stranger would have sworn that I'd just undergone facial surgery. Raddled, that's the word that Clifford had used. Did I look raddled? Maybe tense, overtaut (like the strings of an antique fiddle?), but more gauntly beautiful than raddled, surely. It was all in the eye of the beholder, that's what I was thinking. And since this beholder was in no state of mind to be harsh on herself, I was choosing the favourable view.

Yes, I'd certainly lost weight, without even noticing it. Without even bothering to get on the scales and check, I knew that I must have dropped almost a stone. It didn't thrill me as much as it would have done if I'd still been with Adam. I didn't care really, one way of the other. There was no-one in my life to pat me on the back, that was why. No-one to strip me down and admire my nakedness.

I hadn't had a man for more than a month!

Looking at the bed behind me, reflected in the mirror, I allowed my thoughts to dwell on what had taken place there with the Ingrid Bergman look-alike. I was certain of one thing. That girl would be the last one that I'd make love to. I liked women, but not as lovers. Though, by nature, I was as bisexual as any other human being (once they'd conquered, or come to terms with personal qualms concerning this fact), from now on I would stick with men. I found it less confusing, less demanding, less possessive with men.

And I'd give up group sex. I'd had enough of it. I felt I'd

done it now, I'd seen what it was like – lovely, but not for life. Now I looked forward to romantic dinners with ageing barristers, that sort of thing.

But what I needed most at this very moment was a good fuck.

I knew that it had to come sooner or later, screwing someone other than Adam. On my own. That was the worst thing. No Adam to joke and laugh about it with afterwards. So it made no difference at all who the man might be. I'd go down to the bar and pick anybody up, some boozy old bugger who didn't even know what was happening. Just to get this first milestone over and done with . . .

Some time later that night I was back in my room. I wasn't alone. There was someone with me. The figure was standing by the window when I got back from the bathroom. The worse for wear, very.

'Spring?' I extended my arms in an embrace. So it hadn't worked out with Joe after all, my poor child. I staggered slightly.

I was caught by supporting hands, stronger and hairier hands than my Spring's. A man's voice, slurred with drink, spoke.

'Spring isn't here yet. You'll have to be patient and wait.' I nodded several times to show that I fully agreed.

'Probably still working it out with Joe.'

'Still autumn. Be winter next.' There was a silence. 'Who's Joe, when he's at home?' I shook my head, more vigorously this time.

'Not home. Out to dinner. With Spring.' I smiled at this person, it was a pleasant conversation, but where was my drink? There was a long silence, then eventually the man spoke again.

'Who the hell is Spring?'

'Spring is my daughter. Who the hell are you? Not . . .' I hastily made amends, that was rude . . . . 'Not meaning to be rude.'

'No offence taken. You invited me up for a glass of champagne.'

'Champagne – did I? You'd like a glass of champagne?

74

Sure thing. Not chilled, I'm afraid. No fridge here you see. Big one at Cheyne Walk . . .' I wandered across the room, the person sat down heavily on the bed. More a positive collapse than a dignified lowering of the posterior, I thought to myself and laughed.

'Share the joke.'

I pondered hard on that one. What joke was he talking about? There was no joke. Had someone said something funny? I approached with the bottle of champagne in my hands.

'Open, please.' I commanded, and placed it in his hands. He stared at the bottle without speaking for about five minutes. In a stupor. Then he stared from it up to me.

'Well . . .' He spoke very slowly.

'Well, all right then we won't have champagne. We'll have a spot of fornication instead.' I heard my voice from a very long way away, it didn't really belong to me at all. 'Just get it over and done with.'

He couldn't do it.

'Can't you do it?' I said kindly. 'Look, I'll help you if you like. I'll get on top.' I laid him out nicely, like a mortician would a corpse, with his arms by his side and his face turned up to the ceiling. It was an enjoyable little ritual, like playing with dolly.

'I'm frightened,' he mumbled in the middle of it. 'I'm scared of what you'll do to me.'

'Don't be frightened, don't be scared. I shan't hurt you, I promise. Scout's honour, strike me dead if I should tell you a lie.' I cooed this at him softly. 'Why not shut your eye. Don't look, it won't take long, honestly. I'm just going to put your member in my mouth, like this.'

'Ooh. You won't bite it off – I'd hate that to happen.' Real anxiety, he was raising his voice. 'I've got used to having the old boy around . . . silly, I know.' I took it out of my mouth, it was bigger than when it had gone in, quite a bit bigger. I was pleased with myself. I put on my soothing voice.

'Of course, I won't bite it off, you foolish boy.'

'I'm not a boy, I'm a man. I play cricket every Sunday throughout the summer. And I sail. I'm a deep-sea diver. I play tennis. And in winter I play rugger . . . I say, that's jolly exciting . . . I might manage a spot of whatsit after all . . .

Eight

'Mum! What was that *thing* in your room last night?' Spring was sitting on my bed in her nightie, staring with accusing eyes.

'That "thing" was my experiment.'

'Frankenstein, you mean – it was a *monster!*'

'Really *that* bad?' I tried to open my eyes properly, but failed. 'I didn't ever really see what it looked like, I think I dragged it in from the street. On the other hand, it's more probable that I picked it up in the bar.'

'*Mother!*'

'Yes, darling?' I answered her mildly. 'When did you come in anyway – it's lovely to see you, give me a kiss.' I leant forward from the pillows and proffered a cheek. She shrank back with exaggerated revulsion.

'Yuk! You needn't think that I'm going to kiss *that*. Not where that creature's been. I'll kiss you after your bath.'

'As you like, darling. Now, what time did you come in?'

'In time to catch Frankenstein shambling out of the door. You, of course, were unconscious, as any normal human would be after mating with a member of the animal kingdom.'

'You're a cruel child. Cold-hearted. We can't all look like Cary Grant, Spring.'

'Who? Gary who?'

'We can't all look like John Travolta.'

'I should hope *not*. That has-been!'

I felt faint, not up to all this. I really needed a lobotomy delivered up with Clifford's egg and toast, with a weak cup of milky tea to swill the whole lot down.

'Anyway,' I rallied with supreme self-sacrificing courage. 'How did it pan out with young Joey last night?'

'With Joe? Oh, just fine! I'm really pleased about all that.

77

We've decided to have a space of time away from each other. Then we probably will be able to live together again. In the meantime we can do what we like – no questions asked. And I think that's the best, don't you? Honestly?'

'Honestly. Yes. You are both being very mature.' I was in fear of puking up, nothing to do with the sentiments that I'd just expressed to my darling daughter. It was just that my own internal system was in a wayward revolt of its very own. I was ill. Again. The only portions of my person that felt pleasurably at ease were my private parts. Frankenstein, or not, I had been satisfactorily serviced in my private parts. After the initial fiasco. But it interested me, physiologically, what an effect that contact between inner flesh and outer had actually had. I felt better than I had for a month.

'Look, I can't stay talking, Mum. I've got to get to the theatre, no time for breakfast. See you tonight, about twelve, I promised to have drinks with the cast. We'll probably end up in some club, so I may even be later. OK?'

'OK, darling, but don't come back here. I'm moving into Keith and Anita's place on Cheyne Walk. I told you, didn't I, all about it?'

She couldn't remember, but I just gave her the address. There was an intercom system from the front door. All she had to do was press the bell.

Dressing painfully and with slow care for breakfast, I pondered on the happenings of the night before. Would my person, Frankenstein, be present at the breakfast table? More to the point, would I recognise him if he were there? And would he acknowledge me when I walked in? If indeed I wished him to do so!

Searching on the floor for my shoes, I found them under the bed along with the bottle of champagne. And a woolly hat, navy-blue with a bobble on top. A revolting object and most certainly not mine.

But I had seen exactly such a hat on someone recently, it struck a chord . . .

Shit! The ageing road-sweeper!

It *couldn't* have been him. I argued with myself all down the stairs, still in turmoil as I entered the breakfast room.

But I cleared my throat courageously.

'Good morning, gentlemen.'

'Good morning.' 'Good morning.' 'Good morning.' There were only three of them there, not one of them had lowered his newspaper.

I sat down on the facing side, where the harshest light fell. So that all should get a good look if they so chose. And I placed the bobbled abortion in a prominent position near my plate. Then I waited for it to produce a violent reaction from one of them.

A girl called Tess came in with the breakfast tray, I'd seen her before. She always helped out when anyone on the staff was sick.

'Where's Clifford?' I said. I'd been looking forward to seeing Cliff, to recount last night's adventure. To place the blame on his shoulders for not turning up. If he'd been there in the bar none of this would have happened. Perhaps.

'He's not in today. His mum's had a heart attack. He left a message for you to ring him at this number.'

'Thank you.' I sat looking at the piece of paper with the number scrawled across it, aware that all three of them opposite were regarding me now with interest. But which of them was revealing more than just that? Which of these overgrown schoolboys was blushing? I raised my eyes and steadfastly returned their stares, each of them in turn. Not a flicker. In mild desperation I gave an all-embracing smile and picked up the woollen cap by the bobble.

'Does this by any chance belong to one of you gentlemen? I found it just now on the stairs.' I smiled encouragingly. Now was the time to own up.

'Not mine.' 'Never wear a titfer.' 'Hardly my taste in head-gear.' Ha-bloody-ha.

'Well, that's that then.' I dropped the woolly accident on the floor, the cat immediately pounced upon it and started worrying the woollen bobble. Silence reigned as we got on with our breakfasts. I didn't realise how much I'd miss Clifford.

I rang him whilst I was waiting for the small removal van to arrive and collect me and my belongings. I hadn't fully comprehended just how much rubbish I'd managed to accumulate since the return from New York. Unwearable items of clothing, which had seemed great bargains from the Oxfam at the end of the road. A batch of magazines, that I hadn't even had a chance to read, and wouldn't now. Bits and pieces of food for odd snacks in the room, mostly that Adam had left for me to finish up . . . all of it had to be thrown away. And I had always been notoriously bad at throwing away. My preference was for hoarding, hanging onto everything in case one day it would come in handy.

I needed Adam.

I wanted him with me to organise this move of mine. I wasn't looking forward to being in the Cheyne Walk morgue without a man. I was pitiable, and desperate for protection. My eyes filled with self-induced tears, as if prompted on cue. Boo-hoo, I gave into them. Then I moved over to the window, meaning to moon myself into a really morbid mood. Really giving it some stick. But the cat caught my eye. He was streaking across the lawn, in the direction of the goldfish pond, the woollen hat hanging from his jaws. When he reached it he dropped the hat. I watched it float for a second on the surface of the water, and then slowly sink beneath the surface, bobble last.

I burst out laughing. That pond was a teeming aquarium, already the hat would have landed on the scalp of one of its scaly occupants. A fitting conclusion to the knitting efforts of someone's clicking needles. It had been a pretty cold fish, the man wearing it in my bedroom in the first place. Whoever he may have been.

'Sorry about your mother, Cliff.'

'Darling – lovely to hear you. What's to be sorry about with my mother?'

'Oh.' I stopped short. The telephone wires crackled. 'I just thought that you were probably upset. Don't you two get on that well?'

'Wash your mouth out for saying such a thing, Eve! My mother's an angel. She's up there singing with the rest of them. Me, I've got my ticket booked already to Hades. Better company.'

'When did she go, Cliff?' I subdued my voice. His poor

mother must have passed away in the past couple of hours.

'Six, seven years ago. Why, what's all this about?'

'I'd been told she'd had a heart attack, that's why you didn't come in today.' His laughter interrupted me. He always made up an excuse like that. The real reason was that he wasn't up to it, not after last night. An old boyfriend had called round as he'd been about to leave and meet me. Sorry about that, we'd have a jar another time. What time was I leaving anyway?

'I'm leaving now, any minute, the van is on its way.' I wished he was there, standing next to me in person. I wanted to talk about last night to someone who'd understand without being censorious. Clifford lived by the code of casual pick-ups. Homosexuals were better adjusted in that way than heterosexuals. Whenever Clifford felt the need he went out seeking sex, as simple as that. No having to build a solid relationship first that neither party necessarily wanted.

When I was much younger the mere thought of prostitution filled me with disgust, directed at the men who patronised prostitutes. Not directed at the girls themselves, since I could see that it might be quite a jolly sort of job. But it seemed to me somehow shamefully sinful for a man to resort to this for his enjoyment. Now I understood the necessity for the escape valve. A straightforward screw without any of the complicating factors. If I'd known of a brothel for ladies with chaps servicing their clients, I would have been better off using it last night. For one thing I wouldn't have had to get so blindingly boozed up to go through with it. Nor would the bloke! That alone would have been worth it. And I'd have been better serviced by a professional.

'Did you go down to the bar last night, Eve? If so, what did you pick up? Something nice?' It was as though Clifford had been reading my thoughts.

'Nasty. Something nasty. Neither of us deserved the other, to tell you the truth, Cliff.'

'Silly girl. When you fancy a bit you should give me a ring, I've got the most darling boy for you. A real beauty and into ladies – more's the pity for me . . . I'll introduce you. I'll bring him around to Cheyne Walk when you throw a party – you'll be having a house-warming, I trust?'

A house-warming. A forest-fire, that's what this mausoleum needed, nothing less would lighten the gloom.

'What a God-awful place! 'Ow long you planning to stay 'ere, luv?' The removal-van driver had helped me up with my television set, the rest he'd chosen to leave downstairs in the hallway. But I didn't mind. It would give me something to do for the rest of the morning, preoccupy myself, hauling it all the way up the dark stairway. Hopefully I'd manage to fall and fracture my skull, break several limbs at the same time, and end up in St Stephen's Hospital. Meaning I wouldn't have to stay even one night in this house.

'It'll be the bloody bulb, luv,' the driver had declared reassuringly, when the hall light hadn't gone on. 'You wanna get out to the electrician's up the Kings Road and get a whole bag of them. I know what these old houses are like. The wiring's ancient, all to cock. The bulbs will keep blowing all the time, and let's face it – this sure ain't the kinda hole where you wanna be stuck sittin' in the dark. Not on yer tod, know what I mean!'

I did indeed know what he meant, now that I was doing just that. I needed noise, I needed music, the sound of a human voice. I searched through all my stuff on the floor for my transistor. It wasn't there. It must be amongst the pile of belongings that I'd dumped on the four-poster bed. I found it, but the batteries were beginning to run low and all I could get was a faint reception from Capital Radio. Better than nothing. But where was my record player! And all my records! Still downstairs in one of the cardboard boxes, I'd have to venture down the eerie staircase again, remembering that in that same box I'd packed my electric kettle. At least I'd be able to make myself a comforting cup of tea. The fumbling journey down would be worth it.

I'd left on the one light that had been working, it was on the second landing outside the shrine to Jimi Hendrix. Where the crystal-ball and the psychedelic piano held court. This light illuminated the two adjacent sets of stairs leading up and down from this particular landing, but no further than that. So that in order to leave my floor, as I thought of it (a glorified four-postered bed-sit), I had to grope my way down in almost total darkness. Sliding my hand down the banisters I spoke out loud to myself.

'Lord, bring me my brown trousers.' If I'd come into contact with another hand on that banister, dead or alive, I would have shat myself on the spot.

I reached the landing with the light, heart pounding uncomfortably. The door of the crystal-ball room was open – wider now than when I'd passed it previously. Or was that my imagination? Christ, if I was starting to think like this at midday, what the hell would I be like at midnight! I started singing, shouting the words, the first song I could think of, from *Oklahoma*.

'Oh, what a beautiful morning – oh, what a beautiful day!

'I've got a wonderful feeling, everything's going my way!'

Hardly an appropriate choice, Eve, old girl. Self-mockery writ large. You've never felt lower than this in your whole life . . .

Nine

'My word, you look absolutely *marvellous*, Eve! A Christmas fairy!'

'On top of the tree! With the world at my feet? That's how I feel, good, really good – great to see you, Lawrence. Come into my castle. Enter.' I swished my spangled, black tulle to one side to let him pass. The hall light was working now, I'd spent the afternoon and a small fortune in Peter Jones, buying bulbs and plugs and bed linen and pillows. There'd been a moment of humiliation in the duvet department when the assistant had returned to me with my Access card.

'I'm afraid to say, madame,' he'd shaken a dignified silver-templed head. I knew just what he was about to say, but I'd clean forgotten that I was over my limit at Access.

'How stupid of me, they can't have received my last cheque yet. I'll do it on my American Express card instead. Is that all right?' I was scarlet with shame. This was the first time it had happened, ever. Though even when I was in credit at the bank, I still felt fraudulent withdrawing cash. Imagining that the desk-clerk was viewing me with suspicion, never liking to ask for what I really required in the way of convenient change, just taking it all in five-pound notes. So that it was impossible to purchase an evening paper, or take a short taxi-ride without a fuss at the end for not having the right money.

But I was scarlet with more than shame. What if American Express hadn't cleared my massive debt, though I sent that money weeks ago. The slate must have been wiped clean by now. *It had to be.* I couldn't stand a second humiliation. Rejection at every turn!

The assistant returned with a grave smile on his face. My stomach seized up, but everything was in order. It was just his way of bearing good tidings.

'Shall I lead the way, Lawrence – some of these stair lights won't work. I bought new bulbs for every one of them but there must be something wrong with the sockets. But I took the precaution of purchasing this torch, so you won't fall. Hey – that's odd!' I'd been about to say that one of the landing lights, which had *definitely* not been working when I'd gone down to answer the door to Lawrence, was now inexplicably on. But I decided against it. Just as I decided against showing Lawrence the crystal-ball room and the Jimi Hendrix shrine. Too much about that room disturbed me, from now on I was keeping that door firmly shut. Each time I'd passed it on the stairs, the door had seemed to me to be open at a completely different angle. There were bad vibrations in there, there and down in the basement, and just around the front door. I was learning fast which areas in this house to steer well clear of.

But I didn't want to say any of this to Lawrence. He was a lover from the past, one of the three closest to me before my marriage to Adam. I very much wanted him to see that I hadn't changed at all since then. That I was still light-hearted company, endearingly uncomplicated. Was I harbouring hopes that we may pick up our previous threads? Possibly so. Otherwise why would I have phoned him?

'Well, this is it, this is where I'm squatting, Lawrence. In opulent squalor as you can see.'

'Nothing's changed, I can see that.' He surveyed the piles of pearly baubles, copper bangles, amber beads, jet brooches, costume jewellery, mock diamond necklaces, plastic rings, antique earrings, heaped in a scintillating scatter over the small hillocks of my clothing. A mélange of colour. Fragile lace, filmy chiffon, shining satin, gleaming silk, embroidered brocade, sparkling sequins. All of it still heaped on the floor.

'Yes, well,' I suddenly saw it through his eyes, remembering (too late) the meticulous order in which he chose to live. 'You must excuse the chaos. But I've only just moved in.'

'Don't apologise. I very much enjoy your — 'he waved his arm around the mess, 'your chaos, as you call it. I

85

always have. It reminds me of how much I've missed you, Eve.' We looked at each other. Just smiling. Then we moved closer and grasped each other's hands.

'I missed you too, Lawrence.' I meant it. It was true. I had missed all three of my lovers, they'd become part of my life for those five years between marriages. But I had missed this one the most of all.

'I wrote to you. I sent you cards to Devon and to New York.'

'Did you? That's funny, I didn't ever receive them,' I frowned. Not really, not funny at all. Adam was always the one who collected my post. My personal censoring service. And he'd banned any communication between me and those three. The cut had to be clean, and forever.

But here was Lawrence, back again. There was a lump in my throat at the sight of the reassuring bulk of him, the same mobile mouth, still upturned at each end. The keen, clever eyes – kind now as they devoured me. Kind and concerned and inexpressively tender.

'How've you been, Eve?'

'Me? I've been fabulous! Judge as you find! You can see for yourself.' I disengaged my hands and moved across the room. 'Now what can I offer you to drink, brandy? I got some in – you are still on brandy, I take it? It's been ten years, no, eleven. Habits can change in that time.' I turned to face him from the same distance of the other side of the room. I wanted to play this cool, desperately so. The one thing I was determined to do was not cry. 'By the way, Adam and I have split up, in case you didn't know.' There, it was over and done with. It hadn't been so bad.

'So I read.'

'Yes, well, those gossip columnists have got to write about something, I suppose. Any old rubbish to fill the page. Brandy, yea or nay?' I held up the bottle of Napoleon, which had always been his favourite. But he was tapping his briefcase and opening it up.

'I've brought champagne. I thought the occasion worthy of a celebration, Eve, certainly that.' We both laughed, the slight strain of a moment ago was passing. I had actually considered buying champagne myself, but thought that it might seem as if I was expecting too much of this first meeting. As if I regarded it as a really significant reunion. And I didn't want to appear that intense. If things were to start up again, it should be slowly. I'd hurt Lawrence very badly once already, by leaving him for Adam. By cutting him out of my life so ruthlessly then. I wanted him to understand that I wouldn't behave like that a second time, that now I was more, more – emotionally stable. And I certainly was that now. Wasn't I?

We clinked glasses, I cleared a space for us to sit side by side on the four-poster. There were, as yet, no chairs in this room. I planned to drag up a few of the ones from the dining room. Even, maybe, the chaise-longue from the ghoulish room down below. But for now this intimacy wasn't at all unpleasant. Now and again, one of us would lean forward to squeeze fingers. So far we hadn't kissed. I felt blessed, blessed and cherished. I was with a man who had known me intimately, who'd loved me once. As I had loved him and still did, but in a different way. What was there before had died, I was gradually realising it as we talked of the death of his mother, of the ageing of mine, of how the recession was affecting his company, how the publishers were pressing for my new novel. We were talking as friends, affectionately. Really listening to what the other was saying, caring genuinely, completely involved. It was honest and close, and as such was balm to my troubled soul. Inevitably, the conversation became more personal.

'What happened between you and – him?' I understood that he couldn't bring himself to refer to Adam by name. 'Or don't you want to talk about it, Eve?' My hand was in his again.

'I can talk about it to you, Lawrence. If not you, then who? I don't know what happened. Probably it's too close still to be able to define what went wrong at the end. But it was gradual. An inept explanation, I'm sorry . . .' His grip tightened and then relaxed.

'Perhaps you just got bored with each other.' Gentle eyes.

'Perhaps we did.' I bent forward and kissed his cheek.

'Lovely Lawrence.' He returned the kiss.

'Lovely Eve.' We both laughed. And I sighed. The desire had died, that's what was missing.

'And you, Lawrence? Who have you got in your life?' I prodded him teasingly in the stomach. He didn't lower his gaze, or avert it to avoid mine. It would have been an insult if he had, as if he needed to spare my feelings.

'A nice person. I've settled down, we'll never get married but it works. I try to be well behaved regarding other ladies,' he paused and looked at me significantly, 'but . . .' I put my glass down and gave him a hug.

'But nothing. Don't be naughty. I haven't invited you here to lead you off the straight and narrow.' And I meant it now, though perhaps not before he'd arrived. But I was understanding that I couldn't relive the past. First lesson. One that I should have committed to memory. It would have saved me much wasted time in the months to come. But how could I have known that then?

'I must be off soon, Lawrence. I've got this dinner-party to go to. That's why I'm dolled up like the Christmas fairy.'

'Disappointing. I'd hoped it was in my honour. I wish I was taking you out to dinner, but as I explained on the phone I've got a tedious appointment of my own. Can we do it another time? Will we meet soon – say yes, Eve.'

'Of course we will, Lawrence. I'll come and camp on your doorstep when this house proves too much, too over-powering. Will your nice person let me in, or does she throw cold water on strays?'

'Oh, you two would get on well. She's very bright like you, with a couple of grown-up kids. She's an architect. Would love to meet you.'

'We must arrange it then,' I said lightly, knowing that it would never happen. 'As soon as I get sorted out here. By the way, changing the subject – do you believe in ghosts, Lawrence?' Lawrence, so rational, so reassuringly of this world. He'd give the right answer if anyone would.

'Ghosts? Of course I believe in them. At least – I acknowledge their existence, as I would respond to any presence, palpable or otherwise. Not to do so would surely be impolite.'

A pompous reply, unexpected too. And not the one that I needed to hear.

I left the dinner-party before midnight to be back in time for Spring. The host and hostess and the other guests tried to persuade me to stay, but I would have left anyway. The evening had served its purpose, it had been pleasant enough but anything would have done just to get me out of the house. To avoid all those hours in there on my own.

I dreaded entering it again. But I was fortunate, the taxi driver was a garrulous Glaswegian, reluctant to let me go.

'Kind of a fancy-dress type doo yoo bin too, haff yoo? Yoo luke rreel goot too me, lass. Goot enough to eat!'

I toyed with the idea of asking him in, and would have done so when he asked if there was a chance of a cup of coffee. But I was expecting Spring back at any moment and felt unwilling to have her wrath heaped on my head for another man in my bedroom, a second night in succession. And I knew perfectly well what the coffee would lead to from the expectant manner of this man. The wave-lengths were buzzing, he could sense a certain desperation in me. So I reluctantly replied in the negative. Undaunted, he gave me his name. He might drop in another night, now that he knew where I lived. Jock. I was to remember that he was called Jock. I promised to slot it into my memory bank.

The house was oppressively silent when I went in, it received me with the same disapproval as the spinster aunt that my sister and I had stayed with on seaside holidays as children. We'd come back flushed with the excitements of the fun-fair, but within seconds it would all evaporate, our youthful high spirits. Our happiness. And now, cheered by my human encounter with Jock, I felt the same. Instantly drained of that flaring optimism, reduced to coping with the surrounding gloom.

'You bugger!' I swore at the hall light. The new bulb wouldn't switch on, though I'd left it burning on my departure so that it should greet me on my return. 'I'll shove your sixty watts straight up your miserable bum – and that goes for the rest of you.' I was shouting now up the stairs. Thanks to my own good sense I'd left the torch at the front

89

door and took the precaution of using it all the way up to my room. As I passed the ghoulish floor, I saw – but was I absolutely sure – that the door was very slightly ajar. I fled, dropping the torch, to the fortressed safety of the four-poster. And was still cowering on it when Spring's taxi arrived. Seconds later the door-bell rang. I'd have to go down again!

We sat on the bed, the two of us, talking and drinking tea. I still hadn't ventured to the bedrooms upstairs. And both of us were too nervous to do it tonight. Besides, neither of us relished sleeping alone.

'It'll be better in the daylight, Mumples. Won't it . . . '

'Well it can't be worse. It's just that we haven't lived in an old place like this before. Only a matter of getting used to it, I suppose.' Why were we both whispering?

We drifted off to sleep, though mine was restless. I was too hot, the duvet was a heavier weight than the ones I'd been used to. I tossed it back, away from my body and fell into unconsciousness again. My brain was teeming with shifting images, all of a deeply unpleasant nature, I knew that. But none remained long enough for me to pin them down, I couldn't tell how I was faring, whether or not there was any real confrontation. But there were voices, familiar voices calling my name from a very long way off.

I woke up. I was sweating a cold sweat, my nightdress was damp with it. The voices were still there, echoing in my ears. But there was more. There was a strange odour, a sulphurous stench in the room. So strong that I felt I should suffocate.

It was four in the morning. My blind panic receded slightly when I'd turned on the bedside light. Spring was sound asleep, a light film of perspiration glistened upon her upper lip, but her breathing was regular and her body temperature was quite normal. In contrast to my own. Now I was freezing cold so that I had to tuck the duvet tightly around my body in an effort to dispel the shivering. The sulphurous smell still lingered, but only around the left-hand side of the bed. My side. I'd checked beneath the duvet in an effort to locate the source, thinking that either Spring or myself may have passed wind in our sleep.

Though I doubted that it would have been me. One thing that I noticed, and remarked upon to Adam, was that when we'd given up eating meat neither of us ever farted any more. He'd agreed when it had been brought to his notice that this was indeed true. And had taken to mourning the fact. He enjoyed farts. He thought they smelt fun, were one of life's pleasures to be shared with a loved one. I hadn't cared that much for them, myself.

So, no, it wasn't either of us, the smell was in the room itself. As if proof of a presence that had been here. I could no longer hear voices, but sat up with the duvet clutched around me, listening. Straining my ears for other sounds. For they were there, most certainly, it wasn't my imagination. And I was wide awake now.

It was as if something was whisking, whisking down the stairwell from landing to landing. The hiss of slippery material sliding upon itself. The rustling of silk, seductively female, insidiously so. It sounded to my over-sensitive ears like the passing of taffeta petticoats, and the chilling swish of – crinolines.

Ten

There was a letter from Leeds lying on the mat in the morning. I'd seen the milkman's van from my upstairs window and had shouted down to him to leave me a pint, with some eggs, orange-juice, bread, butter and yoghurt. That should just about see to my shopping for today! All I needed for a civilised breakfast was a newspaper to read, and I'd organised that yesterday. The *Guardian* was on the doorstep, together with the *New Statesman*, *Private Eye*, the *TV Times*, and the *Radio Times*. There they all were, poking in through the wide letterbox.

'Letter from Scarlett!' I waved it at Spring as she lay in the bath. I'd forgotten what her body was like, it was so long since I'd seen it unclothed. I thought what a difference it had made to her, living with a man. No shyness any more, no self-consciousness at all. She simply reclined, barely beneath the surface of the water, her nipples just breaking through. Pale luscious strawberries, peaking the perfectly formed breasts.

'Jesus!' I gave an exaggerated gasp. 'There's some shape in that body, kid. When did that happen?' She laughed.

'Not overnight. The result of devastating dieting – you see, you said the other day that I'd been overdoing the slimming. But now you see the result!'

'Well, then I hadn't seen it in the flesh.' I sat down on the lowered lavatory lid and studied her. 'Sensational! Stand up, let's have a proper look. Turn round. Great bum too, Spring. Buttocks haven't dropped yet. Mm, a sight for my sore eyes. OK, show's over, you can sit down in there and relax. Shall I bring your coffee in, yes?'

I returned with the coffee and began opening Scarlett's letter. As I was doing so, I wondered aloud.

'Do you suppose it would be construed as incestuous for

a mother to overly admire her daughter's body. Or would one be accused of lesbian lechery. Interesting ethic, wouldn't you say?' Spring snorted unceremoniously.

'Christ! You sound just like Adam. Load of bullshit!' I regarded her solemnly.

'That's your considered opinion?' She threw the wet sponge this time in reply. It splattered water all over Scarlett's letter.

'Now see what you've done, spoilt your little sister's missive. I shall read it out loud as best I can.'

'Is that all she can write about, the Yorkshire Ripper? What about that bloke she fancied, hasn't she got him yet?'

'What bloke?' I hadn't finished reading yet, but I lay down the letter. I'd thought that Scarlett was still madly in love with Sebastian. I didn't realise that someone else had loomed on the horizon in Leeds. Just as I hadn't known that all was now well with Spring and Joe. I suffered another stab of conscience for my self-preoccupation over the past months. From now on I would be a better help-mate to my daughters. A tower of sanity and good sense.

It had been for the sake of that resolve that I hadn't told Spring about my disturbing experiences during the night. And in any case, apart from not wanting to set up a chain-reaction of terror in her, I couldn't be absolutely certain now that I hadn't perhaps just imagined it all. In the crisp light of this October morning, with sun slanting through to the sulphurous zone by my bedside, the horror I'd felt seemed now like mere hysteria. I smiled at Spring and repeated my question.

'What bloke is that?'

'Oh, some loony aristocrat that Scarlett was after. You know what she's like, always goes for the wierdos.'

'Well, I just hope he's not the Ripper. If anyone's a weirdo, he certainly is. No, don't laugh, Spring!' I warmed to my theme. 'She is living there in the thick of it at that hostel. And he's not only going for prostitutes any more. That last victim was a student, poor little thing. I am worried about her, you know what Scarlett's like. She's walking around wearing those long wedding-dresses, complete with veils all day long. White from head to toe, I understand that she thinks it's high camp but she hardly blends in with the crowd, now does she?'

'I know what you mean, but you worry too much, Mum. Scarlett can take care of herself. Christ, I pity the poor sod who'd try to attack my sister. She'd have his balls for breakfast. She's *strong!* D'you remember when she went to bed with that old friend of yours, the forty-year-old. Didn't she dislocate his shoulder trying to wrestle with him in bed?' We both began laughing at the memory of the incident.

'Perfectly true,' I said, chuckling. 'But she claimed she was just tickling him. Trying to get some reaction because all he wanted to do was go to sleep.'

'She didn't like it, did she, when he said that she must realise that when you're over forty if you're a man you can only do it in the morning. Load of codswollop, that, for a start. I didn't blame her for turning nasty. I'd have been a bit miffed myself.'

'Well,' I wiped the tears of amusement from my eyes, 'whatever, he ended up in considerable pain. Had to go to the doctor in the morning. Our friendship was never quite the same after that.'

'Serve him right, for trying to seduce the sixteen-year-old daughter of a friend. If anything is a question of ethics that is, surely.'

'Oh, she did the seducing. He was rather an honourable man.'

'An absolute wanker, if you ask me. I tell you one thing, Mum, now we're on our own we must start to think about organising our social life. I look to you to wheel on some tasty eligibles.'

'Who for? You or me? Cheeky thing!'

'Does it matter? We'll share them out – there's nothing wrong in having a pool of men for us to pick and choose from, is there? You don't mind how young they are and I don't mind how old, as long as they've got money. A couple of millionaires?'

'What's that, my darling – a query or a request?'

'You'll work it out, Mumples. You're a clever old boot – got to rush now or I'll be late. Remember to get extra keys

94

cut today, then you won't have to wait up for me.' She kissed me on the cheek.

'I like waiting up for you. I don't mind a bit,' I protested.

'That's what you think now, but I'm planning ahead. We need extra keys as precautionary measures for the future – once we get this social show on the road. We shan't see each other for dust.'

'Mere ships passing in the night, you mean! Now I get the picture.' I beamed.

'Well, you didn't for one moment think that you'd be playing the role of my little old grey-haired mother sitting at home, did you, Mumples?'

'Well, yes, actually. That's what I did think. I was considering adopting something of dignity along those lines.'

But only for the merest whisper of a moment. That's what I thought when she'd gone. There are other ways, other than the traditional ones of waiting home with a cup of tea, to show that the motherly love is still as strong as it has always been. Neither of my girls had been brought up along strictly traditional lines, not as I'd been. But the caring had been just the same. And was stronger than ever.

I ran my own bath and poured in bubbles, then got in and concentrated my mind upon work. My manuscript was all but completed, I just had to think of an appropriate ending. But I had a reasonable idea of what it would be. All I had to do now was get that down on paper. I'd write it in long-hand, since I no longer had a typewriter. That had been foolish, dropping it onto the platform from the train in Devon. Not foolishness, just drunkenness. Much the same thing really. I planned for that sort of behaviour to be behind me, in the past, and lay in the warm water composing the first paragraph of this final episode of the novel. With luck I'd be able to deliver the finished novel to the publishers by early next week. I smiled, things seemed to be working out after all. Then I heard Spring call, though I thought she'd already left.

'I'm in the bath, darling.' I shouted. She must be upstairs, in the bedroom she'd decided upon as hers. A comparatively modern room, with swish velvet curtains which pulled on a silent drawstring. And an olive-green fitted carpet, with a pretty brass bedstead to the big double bed. A luxurious room, well suited to Spring and her delusions of grandeur. She had always been convinced that she was a princess, a personage of royal blood, who had accidentally got mixed up at birth with parents of the lower orders, namely myself. I waited for her answering call. There wasn't one, she must have gone after all.

'Mumples! Mumples . . .'

'Right, kid, I'm coming.' I got out of the bath with some reluctance, I sometimes do my best creative work, just sitting in the bath. But Spring obviously needed to know something about her room, that's why she was still up there and hadn't come down to ask me face to face. I put on my towelling robe and mounted the two flights, then I was facing her room.

'What is it, Spring? You've just dragged me out of the bath so it better be good . . .'

There was no-one in the room. But it was cold, icily so. So cold that when I returned to the bathroom I ran more hot water into the existing tubfull and climbed back in. Planning to drown.

But I didn't drown, instead I turned on the tiny transistor. A record was ending. In a moment there would be the ten o'clock news. I turned the tap off, there was enough hot water swirling around me now that I was beginning to thaw out again and feel human. I'd shut my mind to thinking about why I thought I'd heard Spring's voice. My overactive imagination again. I was interested to hear the news. When it came, my bowels turned liquid.

The Yorkshire Ripper had claimed another victim. A student. The identity would not be revealed yet. The student had lived in the students' hostel and had been found, brutally assaulted, at around four this morning. The hostel was the same one as Scarlett's.

I couldn't get through on the telephone to the students' hostel. The line was jammed, as was the line to the police station in Leeds. Jammed with other mothers as frantic as me. Oh, why had I allowed her to remain up in Leeds with that maniac still at large! I'd insist on her leaving there straight away – today. If she was still alive. *Dear God, don't let it be her . . . please, I'll promise you anything . . .*

A telegram. I'd send a telegram begging Scarlett to come back to London. To live here in the house with Spring and with me. As I was wording it, scrawling it dementedly on the back of an envelope, *her envelope*, the telephone rang. I nearly hit the ceiling.

'Hello,' I could barely hear my own voice.

'Mother, it's me. I thought you'd be worried. It's terrible, isn't it . . . absolutely terrible . . .'

'Scarlett! You're all right! You're safe!'

'Well, I don't know about safe. Everyone's leaving, all the girls. Their parents keep arriving to take them home . . .'

'That's what you're doing, 'I interrupted her. 'You get on the train today, now.'

'Shall I?' her voice wavered. She was even more upset than she was able to admit. She needed me to tell her what she had to do. The trusting child and the omnipotent parent.

We made all the arrangements there and then on the telephone. The continuation of her studies wouldn't be interrupted, not crucially. There was another college of art, just outside London, with a good reputation which had offered her a place. She'd go there, though she'd miss certain of the lecturers in Leeds. Anyway her favourite one was leaving at the end of this term to teach elsewhere. She'd pack all her paintings and equipment together, all her clothes, and arrange to have them sent down to London later on. This would probably take the rest of today. It would be best if she came back tomorrow.

'You won't go out though, tonight, Scarlett.'

'No fear. You don't know what it's been like up here, Mum. When we went out in the evenings it was always in twos and threes, never alone. Certainly not after dark. Everybody says that the whole social scene has been transformed. The pubs, the discos, the clubs. The Ripper's affected everything. I needn't promise to stay in, I don't want to go out. Anyway,' she giggled, for the first time sounding more like herself, 'you can have just as much fun

97

inside the hostel. We are allowed male visitors, you know.'

'Ah! How's the loopy aristocrat? Spring told me you setting your sights on one.'

'Oh – him. No that's over. Too wet for words. But I might make use of my last night – tell you about him tomorrow.'

'I look forward to it, kid. Take care until then.'

'Hey, before you go – what's the house like?'

'The house? Wait and see for yourself . . . it's – different, I have to say that!'

The telephone rang as soon as I'd replaced the receiver. It was Patience, inviting me to lunch.

'I'd heard you'd moved to Cheyne Walk. It's the Stones' house, isn't it? Adam told me yesterday, I go swimming with him every day.'

I was speechless, not at the fact that she went swimming with Adam every day (though I thought that pretty odd), but that it was Adam who'd told her of my move. I'd given strictest instructions at the Chelsea Arts Club not to reveal my whereabouts to Adam, especially not my phone number, and they were usually scrupulous about that. I couldn't believe that they'd let me down. It wasn't that I wanted to play a game of hide-and-seek with him, but that I still didn't trust myself where Adam was concerned. Not yet. I was still vulnerable and was certain that he was too. Later on it might be easier to meet.

'How did you get this number?' I was curious, I needed to know.

'The Chelsea Arts gave it to me, I said we were friends. They didn't give it out too readily. You have a very good security screen working on your behalf there, Eve.'

'How did Adam know I'd moved here then?' I persisted.

'Hey, you sound paranoic. A spot of lunch is what you need. Now where would you prefer, here at the house? Or around the corner in a restaurant?'

I chose the restaurant, though I wasn't hungry. I couldn't eat any of the stuff I'd bought from the milkman after all. The only thing I could get down past my throat was the tea, liquid sustenance. Anything solid formed into an indigestible boulder between my breasts, then seemed to disintegrate into devastating attacks of diarrhoea. My constitution had transformed into that of a camel. I only looked forward to taking liquid aboard at this lunch to see me through the day.

But I chose the public safety of a restaurant because I knew how I'd be with Patience. Though I wanted to see her I'd been putting it off, as one puts off people with whom you have to be completely honest. And Patience was one of those. Tabby was another. If I found myself in Patience's kitchen, that womb, I wouldn't know how to leave. Certainly not to come back to this nightmare of a home.

In any case I'd cry too much.

'One o'clock. Don't worry if you're late. I'm in the middle of a marvellous book, you must borrow it when I finish reading it. I'll be waiting for you in the restaurant with my head stuck in the pages. You'll know which head, I've still got the same hairstyle. Remind me to talk to you about that.'

I didn't weep until we were at the pudding stage, and even then they were discreet tears, sliding like slim transparent slugs over the surface of my cheeks. Plopping into my out-of-season strawberries and cream.

'That's better,' Patience comforted, 'you can break down with me. I'm sure Adam would benefit from a good old howl too, but he keeps his front up with me. A smooth façade, you know what I mean.'

I nodded numbly. I knew what she meant, but I didn't necessarily need to hear how Adam was coping. It made me want to see for myself, so that we – he and I – could cry together.

'Mind you, I'm not in too good a shape either. I needed this lunch. I'm going quietly mad. I haven't heard from Gareth for almost a month. Added to which I'm desperately trying to give up smoking. Do you mind if I borrow one of yours – I see that you've taken it up again.'

'With a vengeance.' I passed her the pack. 'After abstaining for ten years, with the occasional lapse. I started, to Adam's disgust, when we came back from New York. But then I only bought a single packet of twenty at a time. Now I buy them in two-hundreds. Pathetic, I know. And I've given up the daily swim too. I'm kicking the whole health thing. No exercise at all, not even screwing – though I did have a bit the other night. That can't have burnt off many calories. Pretty passive passion, but better than nothing.'

'One of those. I wish I was more like you, but I've never developed a taste for one-night stands. I have to feel that I'm in love. I'm in love with Gareth, that's why I put up with his shit. Can you believe that the bugger could go this long without getting in touch. After a two-year idyll.'

'Has it been as long as that? Perhaps his wife got wind of the affair, or had you quarrelled?' I wiped my nose with my napkin, my own distress diminished.

'No, we never quarrelled. I'd never do it, sink to those domestic depths. I only quarrel with Jake. The nastier I am to him the nicer he is to me, he'd never treat me as contemptuously as Gareth does. There must be a lesson to be learnt somewhere in all this mess.' She sighed, her small cupid's bow mouth drooping at the corners. I studied her prettiness. She was forty now, perhaps more, about the same age as Adam. But her feminine appeal was as positive as it had ever been. The marriage to Jake was her third, but was by far the most important. They'd been together for twenty years. Jake met her as her second marriage was disintegrating and his own had split up. It was instant chemistry between them, he was ten years older and prepared, in fact felt privileged, to take on her two children as well as Patience. They got married and had a daughter. For the first time in her life Patience was in love, passionately in love with Jake. But not any longer (so she said).

'Well, Jake does adore you, Patience. He can't be blamed for that. And he gives you everything, Christ! That beautiful house, the one in the country, he paid for the kids' schooling, holidays in the sun . . .'

'Out of season. The fares are cheaper then.'

'Come on – that's only because you feel the need to fly off in the depths of winter to get a suntan when all the rest of us are whey-faced wimps, Patience. Jake must be the most generous man I've met. What about all those clothes he's bought you, those Zandra Rhodes, and all the jewellery?'

'I'm not into clothes any more. Gareth doesn't approve of all that ostentation. I prefer to under-dress now.'

'So I see,' I said dryly. She had a schoolteacher haircut, was wearing a beige drip-dry shirt with a neat matching skirt, and a cardigan in the same shade. 'The best of British Home Stores, I take it? Or am I wrong – Marks and Spencer?' I thought of how she'd been before Gareth, the suburban business executive. Hair flowing past her shoulders, antique lace ruffling to her ankles. Embroidered shawls hugging her snaky hips. A cross between an exotic gypsy and a fragile Dresden shepherdess. 'Before you accuse me of bitchiness, Patience, I must tell you I mean it unkindly. But I can be crueller than that. You look bloody awful. Little wonder you haven't heard from him, the unspeakable Gareth. What he wanted was an unconventional mistress as an escape from his commonplace wife. And what you've turned yourself into is her, hardly a fantasy figure any more! Be interesting to see what she looks like now, probably walking round the bedroom in a satin suspender belt and black stockings, with stripper's stilettos. Wouldn't be surprised. I saw a film with that theme, role-reversal, called *Captain's Paradise*. He got his Christmas presents mixed up so that his sexy mistress received a massive, illustrated, cookery book. And his sensible wife ended up with a scarlet see-through, baby-doll nightie. With suck-holes for the nipples. And each was ecstatic. Good fun, that film, I wouldn't mind seeing it again. Might come on the telly, I'll give you a call if it does, appertaining as it does to your good self.'

I'd made her laugh. I liked watching her laugh, little dimples appeared all over her face, not just in her cheeks. Her big, baby-blue eyes shone. Her neat, even teeth were so white and so clean against the pale pink of her gum. I don't know why I said it, but before I could stop myself it was out.

'Patience, have you and Adam been to bed together yet?'

Eleven

'Mum! Why on earth would you ask her that?' Scarlett
paused before covering her entire face with a feathered
mask. I couldn't imagine how on earth she'd be able to
drink at tonight's party, or smoke. But that was her own
business, not mine.

Spring, more intrigued with really good gossip, came
straight to the point. Still pouring herself into the cream
satin sheath, a skin-tight essential for her Marilyn Monroe
image.

'Well, have they? What did Patience say?'

'The answer to your first question, Spring, may not
necessarily be found in the answer to your second. Right,
Mum?' Scarlett looked at me with satisfied triumph. She
prided herself on the perceptiveness regarding the de-
viousness of the human race – she could have taken a
degree in it.

'Don't be so bloody obtuse, Scarlett! This isn't an intellectual exercise. I just want to find out if my step-father has
been fucking my mother's best friend, that's all. What did
she say, Mumples – yes or no?'

'She said it wasn't like that between them.' I perched a
David Shilling doughnut on the side of my head, a shimmering confection of silver-lamé and sumptuous velvet.
'That their attachment to each other was based on better
things.'

'Aha – the mystery thickens! The truth, however, fails
to unfold!' Scarlett struck a theatrical pose, mask held
high.

'Shove your face in your feathers and shut up, Scarlett!
What do you think then, Mumples? Do you think they've
done it? And – ' Spring looked over at me with sudden
youthful compassion, 'would you mind if they had?'

102

'I won't mind if you have, Patience. Believe me.' I'd regretted the question as soon as I'd seen the utter consternation on her face, the fading laughter, the dying smile. And I'd continued in less urgent tones, relaxing back in my chair to further the point. 'After all, Adam's hardly going to take up celibacy, is he? It's not his style. And though I'm not going to be having any say in who he chooses to screw from now on, I'd sooner it be someone like you. A friend. You understand what I mean.'

But she hadn't understood. She wanted to make it clear that casual screwing, as I put it, wasn't what appealed to her. And certainly not with friends, where was the love in that?

'There is this difference between us, Eve. You're like Jake, perfectly at home with promiscuity. He picks up people, goes to bed with them, kisses them goodbye, and is quite happy never to see them again. I find it sordid, it would depress me, I'd feel absolutely awful in the morning. I know I would. I'd prefer mooning over the telephone, praying that Gareth will ring.'

'Well, I suppose there is more dignity in that.' I didn't intend any irony.

'Nothing to do with dignity. I just like being in love. I enjoy thinking about him when I'm doing things around the house, it gives me something to look forward to, hoping I'll get a letter. When I sit down with a coffee, or if I pour a drink for myself when I'm alone, I go over in my mind the last time we made love. I don't know how I'd survive if I didn't have that. It's all right for you and Jake, you've got your work. That's what you really love, neither of you have ever really needed another human being. And I need to be needed, Eve.' There was a bitterness in her now. Besides plaintiveness.

'What you *need*, Patience, is to work, start painting again. Why did you ever stop? You were good, really good.'

'That's what Adam's been saying to me since we've started swimming. We talk about it a lot. You see, Eve, we don't all just have sex on our mind like you and Jake. And by the way, since you're being so generous with your husband, I'll be the same with mine. I couldn't care less if you have him.' Her dimples sprang into action again and she gave a throaty laugh. 'Might do some good, you never know, if I thought you two fancied each other. We haven't slept together for ten years, not even in the same bed. There, you didn't know that, did you! Now you see why I need Gareth. I say, do you think you could do me a favour? Come back to the house with me now and telephone his office. I'd like to know if he's dead or alive. You can pretend to be something in aero-nautical engineering.' I decided to be something in shipping.

Spring perched herself at the very edge of the cab seat with her legs stretched out to reduce the creasing of her sheath. I crouched beside her to escape the lethal ostrich additions which Scarlett had fixed, last minute, to her mask. I understood that my right eyeball might make her an amusing and original extra accessory, but I couldn't imagine how I'd manage myself without it for the rest of the evening. Spring continued our earlier conversation.

'Do you mean it, that you would wouldn't mind? You must be a saint, Mumples. I can't *bear* the thought of Joe in bed with somebody else.'

'Mind over matter.' A muffled voice came through the mask. Spring nudged me and began to giggle. 'What sort of evening does she think she's going to have? Not many men want to dance with an ostrich. And how's she going to drink and smoke, or speak to anybody?'

'They have sand buckets as fire precautions at the Embassy Club, she'll be able to stick her head in one of those. Won't you, darling?' The mask nodded vigorously. My fringe lifted in the resulting wind. Fortunately the taxi ride was not a long one. We were on our way to Bond Street for a gala party which was being given for Divine, a special friend of ours. A cult figure over from New York, who'd sprung to instant fame, as a female-impersonating performer in the John Waters movie, *Pink Flamingoes*, by eating poodle shit. No tricks, actually eating it.

We'd become friendly at the Cannes Film Festival last summer, whilst promoting the *Andrew Logan's Alternative Miss World* film, for which I'd done the commentary. Divine and Spring had starred in the film, Divine was the celebrity presenter of the crowned winner, and Spring had entered the contest as Monroe. It promised to be a good party, this one. My first party as a single person out on the town.

'Do you realise, girls,' I said to Spring and Scarlett as we arrived, 'that this is the first party for all three of us in our newly acquired single state!'

'I was thinking that,' Spring exclaimed.' I was just thinking that as you said it. Great minds think alike!'

'Greater minds keep their thoughts to themselves.' The mask nodded solemnly by our side.

'God almighty, she's out of her skull tonight! She's been munching on magic mushrooms? She's coming on strong with the spiritual stuff like some bloody old guru – can't we give her something?'

'Bird-seed?' I said, then began posing automatically, flanked by both daughters as the flashbulbs began popping. We'd have to go through a barrage of these before making the entrance. But we'd got used to it all now. And we certainly made an interesting snap – especially Scarlett, my feathered and faceless offspring. The evidence of former fornication on a poultry farm.

Once inside, however, we got separated. It was inevitable that this would happen in such a crowd. And many of the people there hadn't seen me since my return from the States. Certainly not since my marriage break-up. Though I tried to get down to the bar on the lower level of the club, I found myself pinned against the wall on the stairs unable to move up or down. Surrounded by friendly faces all trying to have a word.

It was ages since I'd seen Spring or Scarlett. Then Scarlett appeared at the edge of the crowd, she'd removed her mask and was beckoning to me urgently, mouthing a single word and pointing behind her. As if to warn me.

Adam was here at the party!

'Would you like me to rescue you, take you away from all this?' A deep, amused voice accompanied the smiling face of the saviour at the edge of the crowd. 'You look as though you could do with some fresh air. Come, take my hand. We can fight our way through this crowd.'

I went with him thankfully, whoever he was he'd saved me from a confrontation which I couldn't have coped with. Not in front of all those people, not surrounded by such sycophantic hysteria. With everyone avariciously noting my ineptly controlled reaction.

'Taxi!' He was hailing a cab. 'What's the address, Eve?' So he knew who I was, hardly surprising. But had I met him before?

'I'm terribly sorry,' I said in the back of the cab. 'But do I know you?'

'We met once at a *Tate Gallery* party some years ago, but I wouldn't expect you to remember.' He squeezed my fingers and held on to them when the squeeze was finished, with obviously no intention of letting them go. Shit in heaven, I thought to myself, here I sodding go again! 'You didn't really want to stay on at the party, did you, Eve? It seemed to me that you needed a friend at that moment to take you away.'

'Thank you, yes. There was – someone – a person there, who I didn't particularly want to bump into.' I turned to look out of the window, averting my face, my eyes suddenly full of tears. Then felt the kindly pressure on my fingers again.

'I understand. You don't have to explain, Eve.' We completed the ride in silence, but by the time we'd arrived at Cheyne Walk, his arm was around my shoulders and he was murmuring soothing words. And when it came to paying the taxi driver, he took control of everything, counting out the right change from my purse because he only had a ten-pound note himself. I even gave him the key to open the front door and let him lead the way with the torch up to my floor. After all that it seemed churlish not to allow him into my bed.

'But who was he, Mumples? Where did he come from? What does he do? You ought to be careful going off in the night like that with complete strangers. We were worried. We looked all over the place for you, didn't we, Scarlett.' Spring was anxiously indignant again.

'I didn't look for you. I knew you'd go home when I told

106

you about Adam.' Scarlett was more sanguine. 'And I think you were right to do so. He wasn't alone.'

'Who was he with?' I looked up with interest, bracing myself for the blow. The girls looked at each other.,

'He was with Monika. That horrible thing.' Spring blurted it out, upset.

'Monika.' I laughed softly to myself. 'That's interesting. The pieces of the puzzle fall into place.'

'What puzzle, what are you talking about?'

I explained about having seen Monika at the Antique Market after I'd decided to move into the house, and how ill at ease she'd seemed to me then. And how I couldn't understand where Adam had got the information about Cheyne Walk, so that he'd been able to tell Patience that I'd moved from the Chelsea Arts. But of course it had come from Monika.

'Cunt!'

'Now then, my darlings,' I laughed again. I was gratefully surprised by my own reaction. No pain. No suffering. Certainly no jealousy. I wondered whether I would be capable of jealousy over a man ever again. Something in me said not, that I was not doomed to plumb those same depths, I had already paid my dues in plenty to that green-eyed goddess. She could not call on me now, nor would she in future. It is possible for a human being to control their own emotional destiny and I had found jealousy to be the most poisonously destructive of all my experiences. And the most corrosively painful, by far, in its hideous persistance. Adam no longer had that power over me.

'So let's get back to last night. How did you two get on?' I regarded them with genuine interest. 'Regale me with the gory details. I'm avid for information.' I looked from one to the other. Scarlett volunteered first.

'I had a hunky boy in my bed. I thought it deserved an inauguration.'

'Was he any good? How many times did you do it, Scarlett?' Spring leaned forward expectantly as Scarlett screwed up her face and started counting on the fingers of one hand. We both stared, jaws agape as she then went on to include fingers on the other.

'Eight fucks! In that many hours – you little liar! She's having us on, isn't she, Mumples?'

'Twerp! I'm just counting up how many days it is to my period. I need to get some more pills.' Scarlett smiled to herself, pleased.

'I was going to say – eight times! You could have passed him on to me when you got tired of him. Are you going to see him again?'

'Spring, he doesn't speak English. Why would I want to see him again?'

'He didn't sound foreign to me. I heard you talking to him at the bar.'

'Oh, he's British all right. He comes from Bridlington, his father owns a chain of bakeries and wants him to become a barrister. But he's only interested in becoming a barman and then opening his own club. He didn't understand a single thing I was saying.'

'I'm not surprised. She'd gone a bit funny last night, hadn't she, Mumples. I think she takes after you. I'm the only sane one in this house. How was he in bed, any good?'

'Straight up and down, big chopper.'

'No fancy stuff? Bit of a bore.'

'As you say. But more boring out of bed than in. I booted him out before going to sleep, I couldn't bear the thought of the small talk in the morning. I think he was grateful to be let out.'

I listened with amusement to their exchange. I used to talk like that to my sister after we'd had a night out, at their age. Except that our revelations were merely to do with whether a boy had fumbled to undo our brassières or not. No bed talk, not in those days of hanging onto virginity. What a wasted youth, that's what I was thinking now. Hamstrung by our hallowed maidenheads.

'Was yours grateful to be let out, Mum?' They were looking at me expectantly.

'Mine? Ah, last night's saviour. My knight in shining armour. No, he wasn't too happy. He wanted to stay on for breakfast.'

'Breakfast! He'd be bloody lucky to get breakfast around here,' Spring snorted. 'You've seen how far down the kitchen is, haven't you, Scarlett! What was he expecting, Mumples? Bacon and egg?'

'Possibly so, yes. I think that he's quite conventional in his habits. He's a stockbroker, so he says. But I don't think his father ever owned a bakery chain in Bridlington, otherwise we might have found we were sharing members of the same family, darling.' I turned to Scarlett, and then back to Spring.

'What about you, Spring. You came home empty-handed?' She shrugged. And then sighed.

'Plenty of offers, but I just didn't fancy them. And the ones I did fancy were all gay. Masses of poufs there last night. Honestly London is getting to be as bad as New York now in that respect. Don't you find that, Scarlett? You'll see it too, Mumples, once you start going the rounds. Sure last night's wasn't gay?'

'Not much evidence of it!' I clenched my fist in the air and held my arm up, from the elbow. Then I growled. 'The Eiffel Tower. Bit sore this morning.'

'What was he like?' they wanted to know. I had to ponder on that one myself. What was he like?

'Rather nice, I think. Bloody good lover, sensitive with his finger-tips. Tracing softly over the skin, that sort of thing . . .'

'Ooh, I love that, when they're good at touching you. Joe's fabulous at that.' Spring shivered with delight.

'Go on.' Scarlett interrupted her sister to interrogate me further. 'How was the mental rapport? Let's get down to fundamentals.'

'That was good too. Witty rejoinders. On the same wavelength. Though I still can't remember meeting him at the *Tate*, I must say.'

'All sounds rather encouraging.' Spring was beaming happily, she always longed for everything to turn out right. Romance was her chosen natural ambience. Scarlett was more in favour of scepticism. 'Does he want to see you again?'

'Spring, honestly, I'm going to have to undertake your re-education.' Scarlett's impatience was thinly veiled, though she spoke jokingly. 'You should be asking whether

Mum wants to see *him*. Not the other way around.'

'Is it important?' Spring let out a long and laboured sigh.

'*Extremely* important. The difference betwen passive and active. Between being a sexual object and a sexual predator.'

'Can't there be a middle line somewhere for people like me, or am I to be out of the running altogether? You're getting so aggressive these days, isn't she, Mumples. Anyway, what's going to happen? Are you going to see him again?'

'He's asked me out to dinner tonight.'

'Gosh, he's keen!' Spring was delighted.

'And are you going?' Scarlett enquired. She looked thoughtful.

'I think I'll go, just to give it a chance.' I could hear the streak of doubt in my own voice. 'But, to tell you the truth, I didn't so much care for what he said this morning. He asked me if I'd be his girl . . .'

'Girl? Girl?' Both my daughters burst out laughing. 'Bit corny!' 'How embarrassing!'

'On the other hand,' Spring stopped laughing and put on what we always used to call her soppy face, one which took over when anything sentimental came on in the way of a love-song or a tender moment on the television. 'You could look at it like this. I think it's rather sweet. He must have fallen in love with you overnight, Mumples. I wish someone would do that with me.'

'What's it mean, then?' Scarlett was suspicious. 'Is he thinking of moving in?'

I jabbed a finger in her direction. 'You may have hit on it there, kid! I didn't much take to being told what to get in for tomorrow's breakfast, I must say. Nor to him looking in the wardrobe, as if sussing out how much space there was for his suits. So I said to him that there was no question of me being his "girl", or anybody else's girl. Not now. It's too soon, wouldn't you say, kids?' I appealed to them both. Scarlett was nodding in resolute agreement, but Spring was still unwilling to relinquish the possibility of a happy ending.

'It's not too soon if you like the person. Is it?' A hopeful question. Her sister shook her head.

'You've got the best plan, Mum. Have dinner with him tonight. Watch out if he brings an overnight bag with a change of clothing in it. But beware most of all if he brings his toothbrush. That's really the thin end of the wedge.'

Spring and I looked at each other, exchanging expressions of amazement not only at the content, but at the confident delivery of this worldly advice. Scarlett intercepted our glance.

'It's simple,' she said airily. 'Basic rule of life. One learns from past experience in order to avoid future mistakes. A practical application of intellect.'

Spring groaned. 'Gawd 'elp us!' And threw her eyes heavenward. 'I hope I'm going to be able to survive this experience, all of us living together in this house.'

'Me too,' added Scarlett. 'But let's hope it's just the three of us and not four. What's your admirer's name anyway, Mum?'

'Dennis.'

'Dennis the Menace?' Spring raised enquiring eyebrows, paving the way for the possibility of emotional disaster connected with Dennis, yet determined to extract the best for herself by turning him into an acceptable lovable cartoon character.

'Well, you've both given me something to think about there, girls. But now we'd all best get this show on the road. What are you doing today, Scarlett? And when are you due at the theatre, Spring? Because I have got to get this manuscript finished, needs must, I've got to earn some money.'

We all went our different ways, knowing we probably wouldn't see each other until the next morning. Spring was on a strenuous schedule at the theatre these days, with a play in rehearsal all day, and the programmed play to do in the evening. She'd arranged to have last night off, to go to the party, but this evening she'd be late again. And Scarlett would be arriving home around four in the morning, having agreed to work at her regular holiday waitressing job in a Covent Garden club. They had rung her as soon as they heard she was back in town. And like me she needed the money. Next week she'd be starting at her new art school, today she was sorting out which paintings to take down there.

So I would be in bed and asleep by the time they were back home, but they both had their own key now. No problem. Except mine. How would the evening turn out? Would I find myself with a lodger by morning?

He arrived at around eight in the evening, Dennis, having rung me twice during the day to check whether I was thinking about him as much as he was thinking about me. I was a little cold on the phone the second time it rang. The call had come at a bad moment, just as I was on the point of deciding whether my heroine would go ahead and divorce her husband or gird her loins and give him another chance. But I'd regretted my curtness afterwards and was prepared to be charming to compensate. It wasn't that bad to have someone so schoolboyishly besotted, I supposed, in the midst of my own emotional upheaval. A rock in the centre of the storm.

But I cooled when I saw his case.

'How's my girl?' He came forward to kiss me before he was hardly off the doorstep. There was whisky on his breath, but I wasn't bothered by it. Other warning bells were signalling something in my brain. Scarlett's words of wisdom.

'What's that?' I demanded. 'An overnight bag with your toothbrush tucked in it. I trust you don't intend taking up residence at this address, Dennis.' Hardly an auspicious start to the evening. He staggered back as if he'd been struck, so genuinely that I felt a stab of conscience, especially at his next words.

'I have my jogging togs in there for the morning. I hope you don't mind, Eve, but I usually run five miles before breakfast. This morning,' he permitted himself a fond smile at me, 'I had other matters on my mind.' And he came closer again, putting his arms around me. 'You look absolutely *lovely* tonight, that's a beautiful thing you're wearing. What is it exactly, a kind of ritzy track suit?'

'That sort of thing.' I thought grimly of what I'd paid for it and how the New York designer might react to this descrip-

tion of his silk-jersey, diamanté-studded couture creation.
But that was unfair of me, how could one expect a stockbroker to describe a breathtaking garment with as much
understanding as a company report. I allowed his arms to
remain where they were around me. Then I stiffened again
as he spoke.

'By the way, good news. It's stopped raining. You won't
be needing your hat for the stroll to the restaurant, though
lower heels might be more advisable.'

We took a taxi to the restaurant, *my taxi* on *my account*,
Dennis having refused to call one in the normal way. He
said the restaurant was only several streets away and that
the stroll would do me good. I'd suggested meeting him
there, that he could combine his five-mile jog with the
journey. But counting up the actual number of streets we
passed in the taxi before reaching the restaurant, I could see
why he declined. Why would anyone wish to jog fifty miles
before dinner? The ugliness of my nature was beginning to
surface.

It had started simmering when he'd hung up his spare
suit in the wardrobe.

'Why are you doing that, Dennis?'

'Sorry, I always hum when I'm happy. It's irritating, I
know, I didn't realise that it was louder than intended. I
want you to let me know if anything I do gets on your
nerves. I plan for it to be perfect between us.' He turned
and given me a burning stare, meant to bring a maidenly
blush to my cheek. He was an attractive man, unmarried
still after several long living-in liaisons with various
women. One had been widowed and the other two were
divorcees. Like me, or how I would soon be. He probably
assumed that I had money, that this house belonged to me.
That had to be it. Time to lay my cards on the table, trusting
that his would find their way to the same place too.

'Look, I'm sure that it's time for a little chat, Dennis. I'm
very grateful for what you did last night, you caught me in a
moment of weakness, but those were abnormal circum-
stances. I am usually more capable of taking care of myself.'

'You're an independent lady, Eve. That's what you
represent, to our loyal public, that's what I admire in you

113

and have admired ever since we first met all those years ago.' He closed the wardrobe door, his suit snuggling in an infuriatingly husbandly fashion next to my new winter coat. I took exception to the intimacy of our apparel. The closing of the door represented a trap with me on the inside.

'Yes, well, what I mean to say is that just because I agreed to have dinner with you doesn't automatically mean that we will sleep together tonight.' I kept the rising desperation out of my voice, desperation in the face of his calm reason-ableness, because both of us knew that what I was saying was untrue. We would end up in bed.

'Didn't I please you last night? I thought that you enjoyed it as much as me, you were so warm, so responsive.' He was hard against me now, guiding my hand between his thighs so that I should feel the stiffening of his penis and the tightness of his testicles. His mouth searched for my mouth,

'This is all for you, Eve.' His stiffness grew, he forced me to grasp it tightly, as tight as a clamp. But even so I felt the force of the growth separating my fingers. Then he was scooping a breast out of my blouson top and bending to suck my (admittedly excited) nipple.

I pulled away. 'No!'

He looked down helplessly at the truncheon deforming his tailored trousers. 'What am I meant to do with that, Eve?'

'Run it under the cold tap. It's the one on the right. But you probably remember the lay-out, you're getting pretty familiar with the place.' (My God, Eve – you're an emas-culating monster when you want to be!) 'While you're downing the dog, I'll be getting my coat on. The cab'll be here any moment. I'll see you by the front door, Dennis.'

The restaurant was noisily casual, a middle-class bistro with carafes of house wine, scrubbed pine-wood benches, many 'Hooray Henry's', and the menu scrawled in chalk up on a blackboard at the far wall. It would have been an ideal meeting spot for lunch between shopping with a female friend. I was decidely overdressed

That didn't worry me as much as the lighting, hardly

suitable for ageing beauties. But at least dampening to the ardour of diners, inclined to hand-holding intimacy. Horrendously similar to the Chinese take-away in High Holborn. I resigned myself to having to depend on my companion when it came to ordering from the blackboard menu, not being able to fathom a word from this distance. I cursed my vanity for leaving my spectacles at home.

'Is the place to your liking, Eve? I come here quite often, I find it unpretentious. And cheap, good value for money.'

'Must be,' I said faintly. (Then to myself, rally round, you over-sophisticated little snotball.) 'Nice and hot in here. I think I'll take off my hat.' I clawed at the frivolous Shilling spangles adorning my carefully arranged curls. Three-quarters of an hour's preparation poured down the drain, destroyed in the passing of a second. But not quite.

'Eve Lynn, darling! How wonderful to see you again after all these years. You won't remember me. It's Mandy Woods's mother, Melanie. You may recall we used to meet at those *ghastly* parent-teacher meetings – and for those hilarious carol concerts the kids put on at the Kensington Kindergarten . . .'

I stared blankly up at the tall redhead gushing over me, struggling for politeness's sake to salvage something familiar in her raddled features (so *that's* what Clifford had meant by raddled, I shrank from the thought that this look might be mine). Trying to go back something like sixteen years when little Mandy Woods would have been at school with Scarlett. For I remembered the child, a stammerer and deeply disturbed by it. Little wonder with this harridan of a mother.

'I recognised you the minute you came in, Eve – well, of course I did. Haven't you done well, photographs everywhere, on the television, and all those books! I tell everyone that we were friends. No-one believes me. Why should they? Why would they believe I'd known anyone famous like you. I've done nothing myself. Oh, but we have one thing in common. I got a divorce from Mandy's father, and my second marriage is on its last legs. Another failure, just like your two marriages. So we're not so different after all . . .'

115

She was *very* drunk. I felt a surge of sympathy for her, I did actually understand what she was going through. She was right, we had something in common. I glanced at Dennis, he was gazing up at the redhead. Enraptured.

'There's the bastard. There's the cold fish. The man I'm about not to be married to – there at the bar.' She swayed and nearly fell right across our scrubbed-pine bench. Dennis, who had risen to his feet at her arrival in true gentlemanly fashion, caught her skilfully by the elbow.

'Would you care to sit with us,' he said it silkily. It occurred to me that he must have made a habit of rescuing damsels in distress. He'd got it off to a fine art. She was as grateful to his kindness now as I had been last night.

'I won't stay, I can see that you are all set for a *tête-à-tête*. Good on you, Eve, baby. You always had that get-up-and-go. Sod all men, sod the swine. Here's to discarded wives, Eve, sister solidarity!' She lifted the glass in her hand, the one that she had brought over with her. I suddenly realised that we had none of our own, nothing to toast with. She realised it too.

'What are you two drinking? Champagne? Yes, of course you're drinking champagne, you're the champagne type. So am I but no bugger seems to realise it. No bugger ever has. Look at this . . .' She thrust her engagement finger under our noses. It was one of the largest diamonds that I'd ever seen outside a shop window. Actually being worn on a human hand.

'He gave that to me. Wants to get rid of me. Promises me the earth in alimony, just so that he can run off and marry his little tart. Good riddance, I say! But he's going to have to fork out the earth. Waiter, two bottles of champagne for this table. My husband's paying, you know him. That pig at the bar.'

I looked helplessly at Dennis as she reeled over to the bar, presumably to inform her husband that he had just bought champagne for two complete strangers.

'I'm sorry, I honestly can't remember her. It looks as if we are going to be landed, however. Do you want to go now? We needn't drink her champagne.' I was ready to leave. What I didn't need was this poor creature. Did I appear as desperate as this to other people?

'I think she's quite fun. She's got the same spirit as you, Eve.' I looked at him to see if he was being serious. He was, perfectly serious. (Christ!)

'You want to stay then, Dennis.' It wasn't a question, because I knew what the answer would be.

'Well, I've never been known to say no to champagne. Besides it would be rather rude to go now, rather unkind. That's not like you, Eve.'

He'd got me there. The bastard. It would have been unkind, and completely out of character for me to have got up and left her there with her pig of a husband – who in any case was probably a perfectly decent human being. And I was a writer after all, wasn't this part of my function to observe the disintegration of the soul and spirit and moral strength of the individual. Except that what I wanted to witness now was optimism, the joy of life, the irrepressible force of natural vitality and intellectual vigour. What I didn't want was to be at this table. But I stayed. The decision to stay was my own. What occurred afterwards could not be blamed upon anybody else.

The husband joined us at one point. I felt sorry for him at the start and then, gradually, I felt myself alienated. Theirs was very clearly a sado-masochistic relationship, but even so I could not believe that his deliberately vicious taunts might pass as verbal love-play. Or that she could possibly relish them. But then that was the whole point of their marriage. I wondered if it would really break up, since one seemed to be giving the other what they both needed.

'Look at her, the drunken slag! She was quite a beauty when I met her. The wife of one of my partners. The business suffered when we ran off together, when I think of the professional suicide I committed for you . . .'

'Yes! When I think of all the virile men I turned down for you. Show them what you have in there. If you can find it. Eve, you'll like this, you can write about it. I bet Dennis has more in his pants . . . hey, yea, or you wouldn't be out with him. And who can blame you. Ooh, I'm so *frustrated* I could climb Nelson's Column and just sit wriggling, right on top of it . . .'

117

'That would be London's loss. Never see the column again. A public monument lost to posterity up your Canyon's Passage.' He leaned towards me, pleased with himself. 'You're supposed to be a writer. Did the alliteration meet with your approval?'

'The alliteration was splendid,' I answered coolly. 'The underlying sentiments are suspect.'

'Not to say chauvinist, what, Eve?'

'I'd agree with you there, Melanie.' Dennis had decided to put in his spoke. 'Bit strong, old chap, that! As a life-long admirer of the female species – splendid creatures, all of 'em – I must spring to the lady's defence.'

'Well, you haven't been there, "old chap". If you had you'd understand what I'm talking about. Melanie may look like a lady, but she's a whore. Aren't you, dearest wife?'

In answer to that, Melanie decided to take dramatic action. Looking back afterwards, I realised that it was from then on that the evening started to spiral.

She took one long and measured look at him, of absolute loathing, then she languorously lifted one leg and placed it on the table. Followed by the other. As she parted her knees her skirt fell back to reveal her smooth, salaciously open thighs. There were only a few couples left in the restaurant now and they were seated some distance away. We at our table were the only ones able to see that she was wearing nothing beneath her skirt, nothing at all. She looked down at herself lovingly, sliding slim, scarlet-nailed fingers from the tip of her toes all the way to the top. They were undeniably elegant legs, indicating in what good condition the rest of her body must be. But it was this very elegance that made her next action appear even more deliberately vulgar.

'Here it is – my snatch! The source of all the trouble. Take a look, Dennis. What do you think, Eve?' She parted the pubic hair and located the nub of her clitoris. 'It's a pretty little pussy, though I say so myself.' Then she began savagely masturbating.

'For God's sake! Melanie! You *disgust* me! I've had enough . . .' The husband stood up and stormed out of the restaurant. We were left at the table, Dennis and I, still mesmerised by Melanie, unable to take our eyes away. But a moment later it seemed as if what had taken place might have been a figment of our imagination. She'd stopped feverishly feeling herself, her hands were no longer between her legs and her feet were back on the floor. The only evidence that anything untoward had taken place was in her manner and in the flushed, triumphant expression on her face.

'That's him out of the way,' she was whispering excitedly. 'Now we three can go off and have a little party of our own . . .'

My resentful reluctance to play any part in this was plainly obvious from the start, as obvious as Dennis's enthusiasm.

'Right,' I said, when we were in the taxi, 'you two keep this cab on, just drop me off at my place.' My voice was sweet, but inside I was seething again. The events of the entire evening had overtaken me. We hadn't eaten anything at all, simply consumed bottle after bottle of champagne. Melanie had called for more after her husband's departure and now I was dizzy with drink. Nevertheless determined not to be manipulated into doing anything I didn't want to do.

Like letting either of them kiss me in the cab.

How was it then that I'd allowed them into the house? And where was I when each of them had been undressing? I sat, fully clothed myself, reading the *Radio Times* with my spectacles set at a rakish angle over my nose. In front of me, behind the television, four buttocks were bobbing around on top of the four-poster bed. On top, it gradually dawned on me, *on top of my brand-new Peter Jones duvet cover!* That pristine piece of prized bed-linen that I'd paid for so anxiously, with such trepidation, on my American Express. My spectacles fell off my face, my head jerked up with such fury. I looked around for a broom with which to beat those bodies off my bed. Then I heard Melanie whinnying.

'Eve, I want Eve. Bring her over to me, Dennis. It's Eve I want to make love to. It's her I want to fuck . . . she'll make me come . . . she'll do it . . . she's so sexy . . .'

'Come on, Eve. Don't be a spoilsport.' Dennis was shouting over his shoulder, still pumping. Now that I was standing I could see just exactly what was going on. But my path was clear, it led not to the bed but away from it. Straight to the wardrobe and Dennis's suit.

I'd never flung a toothbrush out of a window before, but watching it follow Dennis's suit, jogging togs, case, Melanie's discarded clothing and his own, I was interested in what weightlessness there is in a plastic toothbrush. How just that one gust of sudden wind had swung it off-course so that now, peering over, I could just about see it perched half-way up the house, caught in the clasping tendrils of the honeysuckle. I supposed that it must remain there as a constant reminder to me of Melanie. And Dennis. But now I must go downstairs and unlock the front door for these two nudes, so that they could start searching for their stuff in the street.

Twelve

'I need you.'

'You? *You* don't need anybody, Eve.

'I do. I need you, Patience. You say you need to be needed, well, here I am. I've gone down, I'm in decline. I can't deal with this house, and because of that I can't concentrate on what I'm trying to do. Everything's too difficult, the novel's still not finished. Do you know what – I've taken to staying in bed all day. Just sleeping.'

'That's not like you.'

'No, it's not.'

'I'll be over in an hour. Get the kettle on, we'll have a cup of tea.'

I lay back in the four-poster staring into space, I doubted very much if I could get the kettle on. I was incapable of such an effort, dragging myself across the room to the lavatory was about as much as I could manage. And last night had been a bad night, the worst so far. I'd had to keep the lights on until this morning, making a pretence at reading, though seconds after turning the page I couldn't remember a single word on it. I was completely alone in the house and had been for almost a week. Spring was touring with one of the productions, and Scarlett was spending each week now in a cottage with friends, near to her college and only returning to London at weekends.

It was because of Scarlett's reaction to this house that my own had become intensified. So it wasn't just my imagination after all. Her revelations both reassured, and further disturbed me.

'I heard voices last night. I was petrified. I wanted to come down to you but I was too scared.'

'Voices? What sort of voices?' I'd given nothing away, never mentioned my own experiences or my fears.

'Difficult to pin down what sort of voices, but they sounded so familiar that I woke up. I thought you were calling me, or Spring was. I mean they were calling my name. It was horrible, I felt as though there were people in the room standing by the bed. Staring at me. Perhaps it's that room. I think it's haunted, Mum.'

She looked so stricken that I made light of it and laughed, putting my arm around her.

'It's not just that room, kid. I think it's all through the bloody house, but just seems worse in certain bits. You want to try sleeping in this four-poster to really shit yourself!'

'You've heard voices too? Why didn't you say, then I'd have known what to expect.'

I sighed. 'I had to make sure it wasn't me being neurotic, I'm hardly on a very even keel these days, after all.'

'Christ – that's all we need, shitty ghosts sidling around when we're sleeping! Though come to think of it, the other day I thought I heard someone on the stairs and that was at lunchtime.'

'Maybe one of them had come out for a spot of sustenance. What did it sound like?'

'Sort of slithery, like a long skirt on the stairs.'

'I've heard that. I thought it sounded like crinolines.'

We looked at each other, with sober expressions now. 'What can we do?' Scarlett's voice had dropped to a whisper and listening to the fear in it I had the uncanny feeling that others were listening to it too. My scalp slowly shifted. But by a gigantic effort of will I made myself speak normally.

'Do? All we can do, darling, is either move out or learn to live companionably alongside them.'

But to do that needed strength. And mine seemed to be ebbing away.

I'd bumped into Bianca at Ricci Burns, where we were both having our hair done.

'I hear you're living in Anita and Keith's house. I hate that place, it's absolutely horrible. I could never stand it.' She'd shuddered. 'And that four-poster bed, you're not sleeping in that?' When I'd nodded she said, seeming to

122

mean it. 'You'll go out of your mind.'

Marianne Faithful had said the same, expressed positive horror when I'd invited her around. 'I couldn't step foot in that house again. Bad things have happened there, it holds too many appalling memories.'

I'd rung Anita in the States, she was intrigued to hear what I thought of the house.

'I hear voices,' I told her. 'And strange noises on the stairs.'

'What sort of noises?'

'They sound to me like crinolines. Does that sound crazy?'

'Not crazy. I heard them too. But . . .' she paused. 'Remember that if they are ghosts they can do you no real harm, no physical damage.'

'What about mental damage?'

She'd laughed. 'You'll be all right. You'll drive them away if anyone can. Always remember – *you're strong.*'

Correction necessary there – *was* strong. I didn't feel strong any more.

I'd seen Adam twice. Both times he'd been with Monika, and a boy (the homosexual who'd barely tolerated me in our bed). And both times we'd ended up kissing passionately in a corner. Scarlett had torn our unwilling bodies apart. She'd taken me aside and scolded me.

'You didn't go through all that heartache, and I didn't ring each day nor did Spring to help you through it, for you to start all over again with him. You've made your decision. It's done, you're only tormenting yourself.'

And she was right. Of course. Except that later, alone in my bed, I'd think of the kissing, and fall asleep crying.

Tabitha had invited me around for drinks and we'd gone out to dinner. 'Tell me what did you feel towards Rhys after your split-up, I mean immediately after it, Tabby?'

'Venom.' She'd answered without any hesitation.

Venom! I thought about it.

'It clears the brain-cells marvellously, malice. It scourges the sentimental memories – so *clogging*, sentiment, darling! Don't you find? Of course you do, that's what you're suffering now, an overdose of sentimental yearning for things

123

past. As your emotional adviser I prescribe poison. A potent mixture of venom, malice and malevolence. With just a tiny dash of truculence, that should do the trick. Try it out on your ghosts first, for size.'

But I hadn't tried anything yet, except going to the cinema and forcing myself to watch two horror films. One immediately after the other. It seemed to me a positive move in some direction, attempting to confront my own terror, trying to diagnose exactly what it was that I feared.

The first film was Brian De Palma's *Dressed to Kill*, featuring a psychopath. I watched it at around five o'clock in the Odeon on Kensington High Street. The cinema was almost empty, at one point I counted and there were only eight people in the audience, but the film had been released some time ago and had done the rounds. It wasn't new on the circuit. I sank low in my seat as the action progressed, the empty seats around me heightened my general mood of apprehension. I began to think that this applied personal therapy was not such a good idea after all. The purpose of the exercise was to reduce my tension, this film was doing the opposite.

The next film, which I walked to with mounting trepidation, had the same effect on me. *When a Stranger Calls*, this wasn't as skilfully made, over-dramatic in its direction, but even more disturbing for that.

It was about a baby-sitter alone in a big house, with a wide, shadowed staircase. I was reminded of the one which I would have to climb on my own when the film was over. This one was showing at the Classic cinema on the Kings Road, I could have walked home several ways. I chose the brightly lit thoroughfare which at this time of night was thronging with traffic. Families on their way home to cosy fireplaces, or on to parties with warm, friendly faces. I could have been on my way to one of those, but I'd taken to turning down parties now. Since seeing Adam at those last two I was hesitant to risk another encounter. Perversely I had come to regard the conquering of the house as my present and most pressing challenge. I somehow felt it vitally important to win, to emerge as the victor, in the subtle (though increasingly savage) battle between me and the house. Or whatever was contained in the house. I refused to be beaten by forces of the unknown. I'd lived my life and achieved whatever measure of success I'd achieved by brave and forthright confrontration.

But the films had helped, both were about death. Violent death. I couldn't have sat through either of them in New York where violence surrounded us, in fact I had not been to see such films for over two years. Even so the house frightened me more than the films. As I approached Cheyne Walk, my throat constricted with panic. And when I let myself in through the front door, that panic flooded my entire being. I could hear music, throbbing and indistinct, but nevertheless there, floating down from the ghoulish first floor. And the staircase was alive, the rustling silks swept the skirting and whisked around the banisters. There was laughter, thin and high. Excitement in the air. Following on from the crude sensationalism on-screen, I seemed plunged into a real world of total invisibility. Yet stronger and more threatening. As I strode (and I refused to slink and cower) up the stairs sweeping all before me, I reached the room from which the music was drifting. There was no music now, but there was something else.

The crystal ball was turning.

I wasn't surprised. Though the hairs at the back of my neck were standing on end like a cat's, I stepped into the kaleidoscope of shifting light-shapes and turned off the switch. It stopped immediately. So did the rustling. As if by this one act I'd gained some respect. The house grew silent again, withdrew into itself. It was the first night that I slept undisturbed until morning.

Then it started all over again.

Patience arrived in less than an hour, but I'd drifted off to sleep again even in that short time. The doorbell awakened me, I went down to let her in. Her first glance swept over me and my nightie, my unmade-up face and my rumpled hair. Then it took in what she could see of the house.

'This is *ghastly*.'

'It is a bit.'

'You'd best give me a tour of inspection, Eve.'

'Do I have to?'

'You do, to see what we have to contend with.'

I started off in the basement, it was only the second time that I'd dared go down there myself. The first being with Neville when he'd shown me around. But I was weaker now, more susceptible to the wavelengths. I could almost taste the terror on my tongue.

'You're trembling, Eve.' Patience took my arm. Her fingers almost met around my thinness. I felt faint, as if I might actually pass out.

'Hold on a minute, Patience. I think I have to sit down.' I sank onto an old stool and put my head between my knees.

'You're probably hungry. I've brought some delicious snacks for us to eat. My deep-freeze is full of them, I've been cooking for weeks. You know what I'm like when I get the cooking bug. Home-made chutneys, the lot. By the way, I haven't spoken to you for a while. But I meant to ring. Gareth is on the scene again.'

It was the turning point, Patience and her organisation of the house. She worked solidly for three weeks and I paid her as I would a secretary, or rather as a consultant. A consultant with the key to the secret of congenial surroundings. She went out and bought lights: table-lamps, anglepoise lamps, bedside lamps, art-deco lamps, modern Italian, giant candles, night-lights, half a dozen torches which she scattered all down the stairs. She bought teatowels, and tinned foods, a Hoover, a washing-up bowl, another transistor, batteries by the score, four brightly checked table-cloths, air-freshener, fly-killing aerosol, Fairy Liquid, fresh fruit, gin and tonic, tinned smoked oysters. She filled the catering fridge.

She cleared the wardrobe of Anita and Keith's sixties gear, placing the whole lot in plastic bags scattered through with moth-proof balls and stored them carefully in one of the many empty bedrooms upstairs. Then she sorted through all my clothes, still in their piles on the floor, and categorising them into day, evening and casual wear she hung them accordingly in the cupboards. She hauled the more comfortable chairs up from the ground floor and arranged them in an enticing lounging area around the windows, the ones with the best view of the river, and the

126

bridge and Battersea Park, beyond. She brought all of her brilliant home-making skills and Mother Earth warmth to the task.

She did not get rid of the ghosts.

'I have to admit that they are beginning to get me down. I rather dread coming over here now that there isn't really any more I can do. Jake is coming to pick me up soon. Let's see what he says.'

She looked radiant these days, Patience, now that Gareth was back on the scene. Serene and contented, like a cat who's been at the cream. I'd been struck by this same expression on the face of Elizabeth Taylor when I'd seen her dining in Sardi's once, with an attentive Burton by her side, right at the start of their (then) scandalous affair. It never seemed so evident in the photos after they were married. As if that overwhelming glow had gone.

'Be nice to see Jake again, I haven't seen him for ages. How is he?'

Patience shrugged. 'The same.' She was as offhand when Jake arrived, so that I greeted him with more affection than usual just to make up for her indifference. Not that her reaction perturbed him in any way. Even the coldness of her shrugging shoulder enchanted him more effectively than the warm embrace of any other woman. And there were millions of other women who would have given their all for a crack at Jake, from their false teeth to their fannies. And not just women either. Spring had a boyfriend once, who had previously been homosexual, and he'd dragged Spring to every show of Jake's. Engineering it so that Spring would eventually effect an introduction. She afterwards thought that was the only reason he'd asked her out, the fact that she had known Jake.

I understood his attraction, it would have been difficult not to. He was an inspired comedian, his humour operated as an aphrodisiac. Though he was tall and gangling, with a loose, lopsided mouth; the wry, bright, tiny eyes of a bird; the definite signs of a sagging belly, he still exuded a sexual magnetism. His charisma had made him a star. He and I understood each other perfectly. He kissed me on both cheeks, whilst Patience yawned and looked out of the window.

'You look your usual ravishing self, Eve.'

'Bloody liar. I look fucking awful. A piece of dross that the dog has dragged in.'

'The luminous spirit shines through.' He gave his famous grin, lighting the whole room. Patience turned up the tune on the transistor, right up, deliberately drowning Jake's next sentence.

'Love this song,' she shouted and began dancing to it, gyrating skilfully between the chairs. Jake's eyes followed her with indulgent adoration. When it had finished, she made a small mou with her mouth of disappointment.

'It's over.' She sulked.

'If you like it I'll get the record. Tell me what it's called, and I'll make a note now to buy it this afternoon.' He was already taking his diary out of his pocket.

'Oh, Jake – don't indulge me! I only like it at this moment because it happens to be in the Top Ten and I keep hearing it all the time. But I don't want it in the house. It's Cliff Richards, for Christ's sake!'

'I see, darling.' Jake put his diary away again and beamed at us both, completely at ease. His wife's impatience hadn't upset him at all. I wondered how Adam would have taken it if I had ever spoken to him like that. Not at all, he'd have left the room. But now he'd left my life anyway, whereas Patience had Jake securely bound to her forever. Perhaps Tabby was right, malice must work. The titillation of truculence.

'How's the haunted house, then?' He'd taken a look in all the rooms on his way up, there was no need for an organised tour.

'Hateful. I think that Eve should leave here. But she's stubborn, she's determined to suppress whatever it is all by herself. But look at her. I don't think she's up to it.'

Jake was speculative. 'This is a Queen Anne house, isn't it? But I get the feeling, and there certainly is a strong atmosphere though not necessarily evil, that the ghosts are as much to do with the sixties as with earlier times. They might possibly be warring with each other, something like that. And your arrival has disturbed them. After all they've had it their own way for something like seven years. Hasn't

128

it been empty that long? Perhaps, if you are determined to stay, you should impose yourself and your lifestyle on them, rather than the other way around. Why not throw a few of your famous parties, that should shake things up a bit. And if that doesn't work, I'd start to think about an exorcist. Might be fun, all that marvellous hokus-pokus. Give you a chapter in a book!'

Thirteen

It was at the end of the second party that I went to bed with Jake. Several months since he had come to the house to pick up Patience. Months of unusually hectic sexual activity for all three of us, Spring and Scarlett. And me.

Spring had returned from tour in a noticeably ebullient mood. She'd started an affair with one of the actors, a married man with four children and a vindictively possessive mistress. A randy rake, hard-drinking, considerably older, immensely successful since his last television series and universally recognised wherever he went.

Through him she had met a prestigious and dedicated film director, a close friend and working colleague of the actor, also married, with a child on the way. Spring was secretly sleeping with him too.

Joe was desperate for the two of them to get back together. He had now decided that he couldn't live without Spring. He'd had one or two affairs since their split-up, but now realised that it was Spring he really loved. She was spending odd nights over at his place.

But since her return she'd been introduced to the star of a costume-drama epic. He was the latest discovery, hailed as an actor of immense presence by all the critics. He had fallen head-over-heels for my first-born.

Scarlett, bored by the quiet country-cottage week-nights with her friends, was now burning the candle at both ends. She was back full-time in the house, travelling down to college by train at seven-thirty in the morning and returning at the end of the day. Her evenings were either spent waitressing at her usual job, where several of her London friends worked too, or else out at the small clubs which were springing up around Covent Garden.

These clubs were highly elitist, fashionable sometimes

for as little as a month. Nobody was allowed in unless they were suitably attired in bizarre creations. Punks were certainly barred, had been for a long time. Though there was still a proliferation of peacock-haired, safety-pinned punks along the Kings Road, they were contemptuously dismissed as being slow-to-catch-on suburbanites and provincials. Scarlett and her pals had been punks over three years ago. They had also glided through what the media chose to describe as the New Romantic Look. That was right out now. She had discarded her wedding dresses and no longer wore white, but currently favoured widows' weeds. Renaissance style, black from head to toe, with a permanent expression of grieving sorrow on her artificially pale face. But I was noticing that a new persona had emerged in the last week, that of her heroine, Edith Sitwell. Much effort was being put into the intricate winding of turbans, sometimes as high as three feet above her face. There were knuckle-dusters on every finger, and fine shading applied to each side of her nose to achieve the authentic aquiline feature of *La* Sitwell herself.

Needless to say, she was photographed wherever she went, appeared on television programmes featuring the youthful cults, had her name and face in magazines like *Ritz* every month. In the image-obsessed world in which she moved she had become a celebrity.

Her sex life suffered, so it seemed, but only superficially. She had no 'boyfriend' as such, not as Sebastian had been. Her extraordinary appearance was too formidable for any normal youth even to dare approach her. Her devotees were almost exclusively homosexual, exotic beauties themselves with their painted faces and costume-clothes. They sprang mostly from art schools, were fashion designers or had formed pop groups of their own. Two were the lead-singers on records which were currently climbing the charts. Her name was constantly linked with one of those, but there was no real romance, it was merely a front for the fans. He had his boyfriends and Scarlett had whatever she chose to drag home with her from the clubs. One-night stands, which Spring and I were rarely privileged to meet.

But there was the beautiful boy, Rupert. He was always

around, he was the one Scarlett and I shared.

I'd had him first, he was the boy that Clifford had promised me when I was leaving the Chelsea Arts Club. Clifford had brought him to our first party. They had both offered to act as doormen, strong-arm bouncers in case things got tough. And things did get tough. The word had got around Chelsea that there was to be a party on Cheyne Walk, that all you had to do was produce a bottle of champagne and you would automatically be let in. We had almost one hundred gate-crashers. They were still milling around in the front garden and outside in the street at one o'clock in the morning. I was scared that the police would be summoned by at least one of my neighbours. Also, at one hysterical point, the sheer weight of numbers trying to push their way in threatened to splinter the front door, just crash it in.

The trouble was that we had combined our groups of friends, so that there was Spring's prestigious theatrical lot, Scarlett's birds of paradise, and then all my middle-aged pals, many of them celebrities. Each of these three groups were fascinating to each other – let alone to the uninvited hangers-on left outside. I didn't like leaving them outside – it wasn't my idea of democracy, but there was a limit to how many the house would hold. And we had easily three hundred already inside. By the end I'd had to take up residence on the stairs outside my room, to prevent people from entering. Inevitably, however, there were strangers there who neither of the girls or I knew. And it was just as well I kept guard, because we suffered more than the usual petty thefts. My transistor was stolen from downstairs, a portable gramophone, a tape recorder, five overcoats, three handbags, a table-lamp. Up to a week later the telephone was still ringing with enquiries from guests about articles which they had only just realised they were missing.

But it was generally agreed that the party was a stunning success. As joint hostesses, Spring and Scarlett and I saw very little of each other. But we met momentarily at one point in the evening.

'How's it going, girls?' Great, it was going great!

'Hey, Mumples, who's that *gorgeous* morsel on the door

with Clifford?' Spring licked her lips.

'Yeah, Mum – real *hunky*!' Spring rolled her eyes.

'That's my house-warming present. Clifford brought him for me.'

'What, not gay?' They were both astounded.

'Apparently quite the opposite. If either of you want him, be my guest. But you'll have to fight it out between you.'

'Too complicated tonight, I've got two to juggle with already. Christ knows how I'll manage it. Might have to disappear in a minute and have it off with one of them to keep him happy, he's expected home by his wife. Then I'll have the other one after that one's gone.'

Scarlett nodded. 'A bit the same myself, keep being propositioned, but I've got a particular goal in view. See, that one over there.'

I looked. 'That one, you introduced me to? I thought you said he was your tutor.'

'So? No law against screwing tutors, is there, Mum?'

'Not as far as I know, darling.'

Scarlett giggled and pushed up her tits. 'Wouldn't make much difference in this family anyway, would it!'

'Right. So if you two can't fit the divine Rupert in, I'll have him myself as originally planned.'

'Christ, yes! Don't let *him* get away. We keep that one in the family!'

I was fortunate to have kept the evening free, but I'd planned it that way. In the past weeks (or was it months – must have been) my sexual life had got a little out of hand. Following on from the appalling *débâcle* with Dennis and Melanie (I might have to get the police to Dennis if he didn't stop phoning me) I'd lost count of how many ships had passed in the night. Three taxi drivers. One chef. Two television producers. One cartoonist. One naval commander. One actor (a friend of Spring's). One child (the eighteen-year-old younger brother of one of Scarlett's schoolchum's). One publisher. One rock drummer. One virgin! One film-maker. One business man (ugh). One shy Irishman. One club-owner. One Arab sheik. One restaurateur. And that wasn't including what had surfaced from my past! Nor the diamond merchant, the multimillionaire. Pity about him. I really pissed that chance down the drain . . .

I met him at a restaurant close to Cheyne Walk one Sunday lunchtime. I spoke to him first, it wasn't the other way around. But he was sitting on the next table and hadn't taken his eyes off me since we'd arrived.

'Had yer pennyworth, mister?' I'd said, *really* sophisticated! But he was South African, I could tell from his accent, and clearly unfamiliar with the childish expression. His companion had been forced to explain, to the great amusement of our own table.

I was lunching with Spring and Scarlett, and a young protégé of mine whom I'd met up in Leeds, where he'd been an art student. He was a brilliant pupil, looked very much like me, small and dark. He could have passed for my son – well, probably my daughter. He was gay and that day had chosen to wear a frock, a pretty, floral affair. I'd been advising all my friends to take note of him, knowing from instinct that he would one day be a star. He no longer painted, but was writing and singing his own songs and getting a small group together to start recording. Six months later he topped the charts and was fêted by all, but then he was completely unknown. And impoverished.

'Bet he's got a bit in the bank, Mum.' Scarlett leaned forward and whispered. Spring caught what her sister had said.

'Yes, Mumples. We've met that chap he's sitting with, he buys things from Dad. He's the heir to some fortune.'

'OOH-ee!' Little Willie wriggled. 'You wanna get in there, Eve. Could be the answer to all our problems.'

I looked over at the next table again, perhaps I'd killed it stone dead already with the coarseness of my approach. Time to make charming amends!

'I understand from my daughters here that you are familiar with my first husband. You've bought paintings from his gallery. May I introduce myself?' I wasn't addressing the South African. Clever. I waited, now that I had broken the ice, to be introduced by his companion.

We joined up our tables. Marty, the South African, ordered a round of liqueurs since by then we were all at the coffee stage. I can't remember what exactly it was now, but it may have been strega I was drinking. I only remember that I drank three of them.

'So what are you guys doing the rest of the afternoon?' I loved the touch of American in his accent. I missed the American accent more than anything now I was back in London. On impulse (and three stregas) I told him I loved it.

'Honey, I sure hope that you'll find more about me to love than my accent.' His eyes twinkled straight into mine. I sensed the girls and Little Willie sniggering beside me, one of them nudged me beneath the table. This, I thought, is plain sailing. But I felt more than that, I felt a tugging sensation around my heart. He was very much my sort of man. When he stood up, as he did now, he seemed to go on forever. He was over six foot, broad in the shoulder with a strong, bull-like neck. And a paunch, which has always been one of my weaknesses in men. Adam had refused to pander to me in this one respect. He'd refused to cultivate a big belly, point-blank refused.

'Because if you're not doing too much maybe we can all go over to my place. What do you say, folks?' He was still looking at me.

Spring was looking at her watch. 'Well, I have an assignation back home in twenty minutes.' Her film director was coming.

'Just time to slip into something more comfortable, sister, dear.' Scarlett kissed her teasingly on the cheek, then she turned to me. 'Well, Mother, what do you say?' I felt Little Willie's pleading eyes, he'd never been inside a millionaire's place before. He was catching the seven o'clock train back to Leeds today. He'd enjoy having something to tell the folks back home.

'Will we like it in your place, Marty? What excitements will you be offering us?' I stared insolently into his eyes.

'We can start with champagne and see where we go from there, come on, you guys, let's make a move.'

I liked that, the masterful approach. The ability to organise, to assume control. Both my husbands had had it – but then so did Dennis. I must be careful not to jump into the deep end too soon with this one, exert a modicum of self-control, keep an emotional something in reserve. The trouble with my passing ships in the night was that so many of them weren't getting the 'passing' point. Too often they chose to regard me as the port in the storm, somewhere to drop anchor, not just for the night but on a permanent basis. As if reluctant to set sail on life's journey again. My dry dock was crammed to capacity.

'Sir, doth thy chariot await?' I was addressing Marty, but his companion replied that he had his car. The companion was a posh nonentity, the sort who brought out the worst in me, typical of Henry's clients. Typical of his friends. That had been one of the main bones of contention in that first marriage of mine. Our differing opinion on people.

'Will I like it, your car? I have to be very careful what I'm seen driving in. I have a reputation to uphold. Oh, no – is *this* it? Never mind, I shall have to lie crouched on the floor. I trust that we're not going too far.'

The car was sleek and expensive, but lacking in style. Like a dull sitting room on wheels. Afterwards, Scarlett told me that it was the new Mercedes, but that made no difference to me, I had definite preferences in cars. The ones I'd chosen to drive had been Morgan sports cars, a 1930s Rolls Royce, Mini-Mokes, and a strange space-age vehicle designed in Italy. All of them sprayed yellow, all desperately uncomfortable on journeys of any length. Except the Rolls which had only done something like one mile to the gallon. Yet each one an excitement to jump into.

'What do you drive, Marty?' The tester, this question.

'Oh, I don't drive. I run a Roller, my chauffeur drives it for me. But I've given him the weekend off.'

I exchanged meaningful stares with Little Willie and Scarlett from my crouched position on the floor at their feet. The car slowed down and finally stopped.

'Come on, Mother.' Scarlett hauled me to my full height, Marty helped me out of the car.

'You're a weirdo – you know that?' He shook his head as he said it, but his eyes were still twinkling (at that point).

'Oo-er,' Little Willie clutched my arm nervously as Marty led us through what looked like a palatial art gallery. I felt

136

my shoes sinking in carpets so thick that only my ankles were showing. Four inches in height lost in less than a second. I'd have to do something about these carpets, once I was mistress of this place. I valued my inches. It was all right for Marty, he towered above me, but I was confident I could cut him down to size.

'Devastating,' I swept my eyes around at the exquisitely decorated decor. 'Only one criticism. I'm faintly disappointed not to have been carried over the threshold, Marty.' I stared up at him slyly. Without a word he bent down and scooped me up effortlessly in his arms, retracing his footsteps back through the entrance. We re-entered.

'How's that, ma'am? I never like disappointing a lady.'

It was half-past three then, we'd known each other for only an hour. By half-past five we were engaged and by six we were trying to decide how many guests to invite to the wedding. I can't remember just who proposed to whom, the only thing that was worrying me was whether it would be allowable to wear the engagement ring which we'd be choosing in the morning (the minute Cartiers opened). I did tell him that my divorce wasn't through yet.

That didn't worry him. He was a tycoon, familiar with divorce, through he'd only had one. His lawyers could rush it through. It was going to be like this now for the rest of my life, nothing to worry about. Marty would solve all my problems. I counted four empty Dom Perignons.

The chauffeur was summoned with the Rolls. He dropped Little Willie at the station, we had to stop on the way for him to be sick in the street. And then Scarlett and I were driven on to Cheyne Walk, by the time we arrived there Scarlett was snoring on my shoulder. It took me five minutes to find the keyhole, someone had moved it during the day. The chauffeur waited dutifully in the car.

I had only gone home to change for the dinner-party which I was going to do with my fiancé. Though he couldn't bear to let me out of his sight, I'd insisted on wearing something of which he'd be proud. After all, this was our first social event as an engaged couple.

'Mumples! You can't wear that!' Scarlett was wearing the Elizabeth Taylor cat-at-the-cream expression on her face.

Her afternoon's passion had been to her liking. Now she was preparing, with just an hour to spare, for another session this time with the actor. I was sitting on the lavatory seat, waiting to use her bathwater after her. My intended outfit was hanging up against the mirror.

'Why not? Why can't I wear it. It's a ballgown. It's a Balenciaga.'

'I know that, you know that. But it's not the sort of thing that people wear to intimate dinner-parties in private houses. You'll take up too much room for a start. You'll need two place settings.'

'I shall sit on my fiancé's knee. He'll like that. We, as yet, have had no physical contact. Exciting isn't it! I shall insist, I think, that intercourse shall not take place until after the nuptuals. I want this husband to have proper respect for me.'

'Is that wise, Mumples? It wouldn't suit me, I must say. You need to know just what you're getting, don't you. He might be hopeless at it, and what good would that do you?'

'No-one's hopeless, not really. Screwing's a skill, it just needs to be studied, like motor-cycle maintenance. It's a matter of learning, haven't you found that?'

'Mechanics aren't my line, I don't go in for them. I like it where it's loving, though I must say that I appreciate experience as well. I was making a list this afternoon in my mind as we were going through the motions, giving different marks out of ten for the best lover out of my current four.'

'Really? Who came bottom? Obviously the one you were in bed with this afternoon otherwise your mind wouldn't have been preoccupied with making lists.'

'Exactly! But, on the other hand. I think he's the one who loves me most, so in the next list I made he came out top.'

'Difficult, isn't it, deciding on priorities? I'm just going to get married myself. Your father was a fabulous lover, so was Adam. This time I'm going for money in the bank, reversing the principle of if you take care of the pennies the pounds will take care of themselves. I've probably concentrated too much up until now on the penis. Now I shall concentrate on the person, the penis can see to itself.'

I sensed impending disaster as soon as I arrived back at my fiancé's. In my absence two friends had dropped by for a drink, but whilst the posh companion had been an inoffensive drip, this couple were downright fascists. The woman was wearing Gucci shoes, had frosted highlights (always suspect) in her carefully windswept fall of hair. Her handbag was one of those with the designer's initials stampled all over it. She'd stepped straight from the pages of Jacqueline Susann, as had her cashmered husband. They were figures from my past, from that summer with the impotent playboy in Marbella. They were talking politics, and slimming aids. How the hunger-strikers in Ireland were doing the world such a service to rid it of such scum, how effective their diet was as a means of losing weight. In moderation, of course.

I excused myself, for fear of talking out of turn.

After they'd left I challenged Marty.

'Tell me, are those two typical of your friends? Are those the sort of shits we'll be dining with tonight? Because if so I think that I'd better not go. I'll behave badly, I know it. I'll disappoint you, it'll spoil things.' He persuaded me out of my doubts, against my better instincts. The moment we arrived at the Knightsbridge mansion and the butler answered the door I knew what a monstrous mistake I had made.

Tabby was there. We sat, banked by so many blossoms that it might have been a wedding reception or a funeral parlour. Hideous paintings hung on the tapestried walls, fake mockeries of old masters lit by sodium-strip lighting.

'This is like sitting in a cross between the Athenaeum and the antique furniture department of Harrods,' I confided to Tabby. 'You'd think that with all this money they'd be able to afford an electrician, get in a bit of decent lighting.' Marty frowned by my side, but I was only just starting then, it wasn't until dinner that I really got up steam.

The conversation was centred upon education and the importance of retaining the public school system. Most of the men present had been either to Eton or Harrow. The women to Roedean or Cheltenham.

'As a matter of interest, where were you at school, Eve?'

One supercilious shit-head dressed in Yves St Laurent asked.

'Scrotum,' I replied. A stir ran round the table. 'You probably don't know Scrotum, a minor secondary modern school, operating within the state system, situated half-way between Willesden High Road and Harlesden.' Only Marty laughed, he wasn't English and class distinction hadn't the same meaning for him. But his laughter was my undoing, it encouraged me to go further than I otherwise might have. And I had now caught the rapt, if uneasy, attention of the entire table. Emboldened I pushed on. Upbraiding the servility of the waiters (who flinched from me, fearing that my frankness might cost them their jobs); criticising the conversational level of brow; insulting the host for gathering together such a collection of blinkered right-wing buggers. Imploring Tabby to take stock of her life and wonder what she was doing with such moneyed dullards after what she'd known with Rhys. And finally pushing back my chair and announcing that I was leaving, I'd had enough.

Marty insisted on leaving with me. We sat in silence in the back of the Rolls. I thought of how disappointed Spring and Scarlett would be.

'Tell him, if he's to be our new stepfather, that what I want for Christmas is a floor-length fox fur and a cocktail watch covered in diamonds.' Spring had shouted as I was going out of the door.

'And what I want is a new paint palette and easel, an account carte-blanche at Windsor and Newton, and Foyles. And all the first editions of Edith Sitwell.' Spring's voice floated drunkenly down the stairwell.

'Will you come in, Marty?' The subdued voice was mine. His own answered in barely controlled fury.

'I shall *not* be coming in, now or ever, honey! I shall be returning to my friends, the friends that you so coarsely insulted, and attempt an abject apology on your behalf.'

I stood on the pavement of Cheyne Walk watching the disappearing Rolls, watching the answer to all my bills wafting out of my life.

'Well, you've blown that, you silly bitch!' I wobbled into

the house and said hello to the ghosts. They were better company than the turds I'd just left.

But in the morning I was riddled with remorse and sent a telegram to Marty, saying just that.

'APOLOGIES FOR APPALLING BEHAVIOUR. SCROTUM EX-SCHOLARS BEHAVE BEAUTIFULLY WHEN GIVEN A SECOND CHANCE. CAN A CANDLELIT DINNER BE ARRANGED? RING ME.'

He didn't ring. Three days later I rang him to be told that he was in Tokyo (where else would a diamond merchant be?) and would be returning at the end of the week, on Friday. I'd been persistent and had pressed for an approximate time of arrival. Early evening was his expected time.

I spent the entire day on my appearance, manicuring my nails, re-touching my roots, doing press-ups, oiling my body, plucking my eyebrows, shaving my legs, picking my nose, looking fruitlessly through my wardrobe for a Sloane Ranger outfit.

'I think it's rather degrading, Mum. This is the twentieth century. You shouldn't be doing all that for a man. You'd be better employed reading Bertrand Russell.' Scarlett looked up from her Simone de Beauvoir.

'Leave Mumples alone. It's all a means to an end. It's getting colder, I really *need* that fox fur.' Spring generously allowed me a loan of her gold chains, and a lavish spray of her Bal à Versailles.

At seven-thirty I rang his number. He had just that moment walked in, he was suffering slight jet-lag and needed to unwind. He'd ring me later, he'd planned on a quiet evening at home.

'Did you get my telegram?' I asked nervously since he hadn't mentioned it. 'And if so, am I forgiven?' He'd laughed at that, saying that the humour of its content had somewhat retrieved the situation.

'Sounds hopeful?' I turned to the girls, they were both going out.

'Wait and see if he rings first before building up hopes.' Scarlett wasn't willing to commit herself.

'*Very* hopeful! At least he was speaking to you.' Spring shivered into her cloth coat. 'You'll do it, Mumples. He'll

141

ring.' I began dressing in clothes suitable for a quiet evening at home. His home, not mine – ever the optimist!

But by nine-thirty he still hadn't rung. Poor lamb, he must be taking a nap. I'd call a taxi and go around there to make him a hot drink and tuck him up for the night, just to show what an understanding wife I'd be. I didn't bother with a coat, nor with taking any money. The chauffeur could drive me home. I'd changed my outfit several times already, once because I'd spilt the oil from a sardine tin that I'd opened as something to snack on with Branston Pickle and sliced cucumber. An indigestible mistake, that, but I hadn't eaten all day and it was all that the fridge had on offer. So I'd ended up in scarlet crêpe, from top to toe, a long dress. Suitably jolly, yet sexily vampish. With a shimmering skull-cap of scarlet sequins. The taxi driver whistled approval as he let me in.

There was no answer to the doorbell. So I rang it several times. The servants must be out, I thought, and Marty must be asleep though it was still early, only around half-past ten. I kept my finger on the bell for the final time, he'd be pleased to be woken by me. Who wouldn't! The door was wrenched open so suddenly that I almost lost my balance in surprise. Marty stood glowering in the hall.

Within six minutes, stumbling along Park Lane, caught up in the late night, home-going crowds, I tried to reconstruct the explosive scene I'd just been through.

'What the hell do you think you're doing here!' That had been his friendly greeting.

'Welcome home, Marty.' He was wearing a dinner jacket, I noted that as I made a move to enter. He barred my way.

'Oh, no, you don't. I'm not inviting you in, honey. I have friends downstairs for dinner. I'm not risking you with my friends again, taking over the conversation, monopolising the entire table, being aggressive just because it amuses you. And, for your information, you weren't invited to dine for that very reason.'

'I've eaten already, Marty.' The sardines were swimming in my throat. I might just bespoil that immaculate dinner jacket at any moment. I stared cheekily at his flushed face.

'So there!'

'Look, honey. You just can't do this – call on a person unannounced. It's impolite. You CANNOT do it!'

'I just have. I've just done it.' My childish defiance over-topped itself. I stuck out my tongue.' That's to you, twerpy – with knobs on!'

Fourteen

Young Rupert was nice, a beautifully brought-up, nineteen-year-old. And spectacularly well hung. When he was by the bed, ready to leap on top of me, his erection reached almost up to his navel. It never stuck straight out, nor (certainly) did it ever droop. But stood to attention straight as a guardsman, hard up against his stomach. I liked it. I liked it very much indeed.

And he was good with it too, had been screwing girls since he was twelve. Girls of all ages, I wasn't his oldest.

'What would your mother say if she could see you now?' I asked him the direct question on our second time in bed.

'Oh, she knows that I'm sleeping with you. We talk about it.'

'Christ!'

'Well, she and I have the same sort of relationship as you have with Spring and Scarlett. I tell her everything, we've never had any secrets. She admires you enormously anyway, she's one of your fans. She's proud that I'm your lover, she boasts about it to her friends when they have coffee together.'

'Christ!' I said it again.

But he put me on a pedestal. That is one of the troubles with very young boys. The worshipping, the hanging on every word like a lapdog. And he perused every inch of my body in mute adoration, every stretch-mark, every sag, every wrinkle, every enlarged pore, searching lovingly through my pubic hairs to see if he could spot the two silver ones which I had assured him did exist.

'You're a *beautiful* lady, Eve.'

'*No, I'm not*, young Rupert.'

'You are to me, Eve. I love you.'

'I love you too, young Rupert.' I'd say it back. Well, why

not if it made him happy. There was a time when I never used the term I love you, unless I meant it. Unless I was saying it back to someone whom I was intending to marry. I didn't want to de-value the word love. Nor did I do anything but believe it when I was told by men or boys that they loved me. I thought that it meant that we would be together forever, barring all others, sacred only to ourselves.

But now I took a wider view of love. Feeling that all my encounters, whether they lasted ten minutes or ten years, one-night stands or long-term marriages, were as so many bites of the apple. Love bites. Some merely bruises on the skin, others going so deep that they touched the core itself. It would take a lifetime to demolish the entire fruit.

'I think about you all the time, Eve.' Desperation in the boyish voice. I only thought about him when he was there.

'Do you, young Rupert? You're *so* sweet, let me kiss you.'

'What would you like me to do to you, Eve?'

'Same again would be very nice, my angel.' I parted my legs obligingly.

'What about me buggering you? Would you like me to do that?'

'Well, let's put it this way – I'm not beside myself with enthusiasm. Another time would do.' I didn't tell him but both the rock drummer and the Arab sheik (each of whom I'd had on consecutive nights) had gone at me hell-bent up the backside. To Spring and Scarlett's great hilarity I'd had to carry a cushion around with me for up to three days. My arsehole was *agape*, it looked like the mouth of a very old woman, with all the teeth ripped out. All sag and saliva. But it was mending nicely now, though I could imagine that another onslaught on that particular area of my anatomy might feel like salt on an open wound.

I'd been to bed with young Rupert about five times before Scarlett decided to take him over. He'd been around at our house with other people for a glass of wine and we were all looking at the television when Scarlett arrived from a consciousness-raising meeting of young feminists affiliated to the group, Women in Media. She'd just come to the end of an affair with a French painter, a torrid affair of the heart (and other parts). He had departed for Paris that very morning and planned to go on from there to live in Madrid. So her eyes were straying. That evening they strayed in the direction of young Rupert.

'Would you mind, Mum?' she whispered to me as I was making the coffee.

'Don't be daft! Mind? Of course I wouldn't mind. What's mine is yours, you know that.'

Spring came in later on, after Scarlett and young Rupert had retired to her bed.

'Where's old Scarlett?' Spring wanted to know.

'Upstairs in bed.'

'Rather early for her, isn't it?'

'With Rupert, young Rupert.'

'What?'

'You heard,' I said. Then laughed at the expression on her face.

'So Scarlett's screwing young Rupert. I'd better have him next – except he's a bit young for me, wouldn't you say, Mumples?'

'Only two and a half years younger. Almost twenty years younger in my case, darling. So who am I to ask!'

'Different with you, more like mother and son. With me it would be as if I was his older sister. Ruder somehow, I don't know why. Anyway I like older men, more to talk about, not so boring. Wonder how Scarlett will like him, he's rather ancient for her, isn't he? I thought she was going for fourteen-year-olds these days, little beauties barely off their mothers' milk.'

In the morning we waited impatiently to find out just what Scarlett had made of young Rupert. Mincemeat probably.

'Well?' Spring and I had her cup of tea all ready and waiting.

'Well what?' Scarlett yawned. Spring and I exchanged glances of impatience.

'She's in one of those moods. You're deliberately keeping us on tenter-hooks, you little turd.'

'Nice thing to hear before I've even had my cup of tea. Lovely way to talk to a sister. You two are like vultures.'

'Cut the crap, kid.' I interrupted coarsely. 'How did you find young Rupert?'

'Good fuck?' Spring came straight to the point.

'Mm. So-so.'

'Really? Only so-so. Our mother gives him a considerably higher recommendation than that.'

'Yes, well, at her age she has to be grateful. True, Mum?'

'Absolutely! Any crumb for the old cow.' I grinned at them both.

'Poor little Mumples.' Spring hugged me. 'I think that was rather cruel of you, Scarlett.'

Scarlett yawned again. 'You have to appreciate my humour. Aggression with the vital ingredient of wit. Mum knows what I mean.' She winked at me, I winked back.

'I hope you were kind to him. He's a nice child, and you must have found his body beautiful at least.'

'Bland. I think I prefer more bite.'

'We'd best buy you a dog. You could go to sleep snarling at each other.' Spring giggled.

'That, sister, dear, was aggression lacking the vital ingredient.' Scarlett tossed her head.

'Now, now, children. Let's keep the party nice.' I put on my mummyish voice.

'Ooh, listen to Mother exerting parental control.' They chorused in unison, united in their mockery.

I sniffed. 'I sometimes think that you two don't accord me the respect that I deserve.' My words were drowned in their spluttering guffaws.

'By the way,' Spring announced when they'd recovered their composure, 'I've got a bloke going spare if anyone wants him.' She was referring to the acclaimed star of the costume-drama epic. I knew because she'd been complaining of his meanness with money for the past week. The last two times he'd taken her to dinner she'd had to pay for the major portion of the bill. His cash was all tied up in the Halifax Building Society and his agent had advised against his having credit cards.

'Yuk, too old for me. In any case I wouldn't want your cast-offs. Even if I could afford him, which I can't.' Scarlett shook an adamant head. Spring turned to me enquiringly.

147

'What about you, Mumples?'

I considered the question. 'What are his other drawbacks apart from the stinginess? That's assuming that I can squeeze him into the schedule.'

'Spotty. Boils on the botty.'

'Bravo, sister. Brief description but succinct! I should think that's successfully put Mother off. Right, Mum?'

'I'll admit that I'd never actually entertain advertising for an acned arsehole. It's not top in my list of physical preferences, so perhaps I'll reject your offer, Spring. Sweet of you to think of us, though – isn't it, Scarlett.'

'Very sweet. Thank you, sister, dear.' Scarlett looked thoughtful 'I wonder who I've got to throw into the pool, now we're about it. I know, that nasty little nincompoop, Neil, who keeps ringing me up.'

'Oh, nice, very nice! This isn't meant to be a *cess* pool, we must maintain some standards, mustn't we, Mumples? He's *horrible*, that creature!'

'Is he the hippie, Scarlett?'

'Yeah, man – he's hitting the India trail soon, so you'll have to be quick off the mark. He's hoping that I'll go with him. Ha, pigs can fly! That's what I told him.'

'Another reject, I'm afraid. Anything else on offer? Anybody want anything else of mine. What about one of my taxi drivers?' The taxi drivers I'd entertained were always good for a scathing comment from either of my daughters. They both snorted now.

Spring exclaimed 'Yes, Mumples – that reminds me. The other night when I took a taxi home from the theatre and we stopped outside here, the driver refused my fare. He said he'd prefer to come in for a coffee, he'd heard that it was the custom of the house. Imagine! I called him a cheeky bugger and threw the fare in his face. Every cab rank in London probably knows about your distribution of favours. I expect they've passed it around on the cab-radio, special announcement.'

'Probably think this is a posh brothel,' Scarlett said contentedly. 'Efficient way to advertise if we get really broke and decide to go into business.' I laughed, but Spring didn't. She sat shaking her head.

'Honestly,' she said, 'you two have got the morals of a couple of alley-cats. I don't know how I manage to maintain my romantic illusions. More sensitive, I suppose, to the spiritual side of life.'

'Bollocks! Marriage-breaker!' Scarlett turned to me. 'Hey, Mum, talking about spiritual matters, I think it's getting better here in the house now. I don't hear the ghosts half as much now.'

'I've never heard them. I don't believe that they exist.'

'Strange, that, sister dear – for someone so sensitive.'

'Well, I think you're both a bit barmy. You know what she was doing the other morning?' Her finger pointed at me. 'I caught her at it. She was going from room to room, standing at the door and shouting in, "Look, you lot – just fuck off out of it! I'm living here now. Got it!" Like a mad person. Hardly normal behaviour, would you say?'

'Well, 'I said defensively. 'It's starting to work. I do it every morning now, as soon as I get up. But I think the party helped, this second one should really stun them into passivity. What a good idea of Jake's for us to give these parties.'

'I love Jake and Patience. I think of all your friends those are the best. And Tabby. Are they all coming, by the way? They didn't come to the last one.' Spring looked up before starting on her nails, manicuring was one of her favourite occupations.

'Tabby's in Cologne, doing a concert. Patience is still in the country. Jake's coming though, that'll be nice.'

It was nice. It was always lovely to see him, though I had no idea at the start of the evening that we would end up together, that he would still be there in the morning.

Several of my lovers were present at the party, but I had told each of them not to expect very much of my company. Nor to hope that they would spend what was left of the night, at the end, in my bed. I was the hostess after all and would be preoccupied with my duties. We were anticipating a vast number of guests again. Even more turned up than we'd bargained for, but I'd taken the precaution of hiring two professional bouncers this time. And it was easy for them to distinguish invited friends and those who were gate-crashers. Friends had been told that to gain entry they must bring either a bottle of Tequila or a carton of orange-juice, dependant on the state of their finances. This was meant to be a swimming-pool party, California style, something to cheer up the bleakness of winter. People were expected to come in terry-towelling robes, or bikinis (top-less if desired), and swimming trunks. Though we had no pool in Cheyne Walk, there were all our bathrooms if any-one wished to splash about and I'd turned the heating right up so no-one would catch cold. Also the mode of dress would assist the bouncers even further.

By midnight it was impossible to move, but then miraculously the crowds cleared and one could actually conduct a conversation without having to shout. I couldn't believe that so many people had left this early. The explanation was simple. An orgy was in full progress down in the basement. But by the time I was told of it, everything was over. The ground floor filled up again.

'I wasn't too pleased about that.' I hailed Jake, who'd just reappeared. 'I'd have liked to have had a look, someone might have told me.'

He'd slipped his arm around my waist. 'Told you what, darling?'

'About the orgy in the basement. Three people were giving an exhibition of a perverted sexual nature. Isn't that where you've just been?'

'Not me, no. I've just been upstairs in your bathroom, screwing a sexy feminist on the floor.'

'That's nice, Jake!'

'It was. Very nice indeed. She's had to leave though to relieve her baby-sitter. One of these one-parent families, just decided to go ahead and have a child all on her own. Quite a remarkable girl as a matter of fact.'

I sighed. 'Great, isn't it. I always find when I give a party that everyone else, all the guests, get to have a piece of the action. I end up with nothing, as usual.'

His arm tightened around my waist. He kissed me lightly on the lips. 'Not necessarily the case tonight though, Eve.' We looked at each other, no further words were necessary. But I laughed.

'You're insatiable, Jake. You've just devoured the first course, now you're ready for the second. Are you sure that you're up to it?'

'I could do with having drunk less, might not be a peak performance, but the appetite is ebulliently healthy – I assure you.'

My mouth was full of his tongue barely before he'd finished speaking, the kiss was a long one. I closed my eyes somewhere in the middle of it as I began actively kissing him back. The fact that this was Jake, my old familiar, the loving husband of my best friend, didn't enter my mind. Not at all. Not until we were upstairs and undressed, and in the four-poster.

'Hold on,' I said. 'What about Patience?'

'Patience won't mind. She doesn't give a damn what I do, you know that. Mind you, I think we should keep this to ourselves, nevertheless. It might upset her, the fact that it's you. We'll have it as our secret.'

'I don't like that. I've never had a secret from Patience. I tell her everything. Our friendship is based on that honesty between us.'

'This can be the first and last secret you'll keep from her. It just is best not to tell her, believe me, darling. I know Patience better than you.' His voice was authoritatively firm.

I should have stopped what we were about to do, there and then, whilst there was still time. But it was too late. His fingers were stroking my breasts, he was nuzzling into my neck, he was levering one leg, his penis was poised in position. My spirit was willing, but my flesh was weak. In the pitiably inequal struggle between the two, it was the flesh that won. Hadn't it always with me . . .

'What are you going to tell Patience?' The girls were concerned, as was I. I was meant to give her a ring today to gossip about the party and who'd been there. She liked getting phone calls when she was in the country, just to keep her in touch with town. I believed her when she said that she hadn't been to bed with Adam. But I wondered, facing it truthfully, if the knowing she hadn't was what enabled me to say that I wouldn't have minded. Easy to be magnanimous over situations when they haven't arisen.

'What do you think I should do, girls?'

'Tell her.' Scarlett said immediately. 'Honesty is the best policy, to make use of the cliché.'

'I wouldn't.' Spring was as emphatic. 'What wives don't know they won't worry about. Listen to my words of wisdom, I'm the authority on wives.'

'Of course, if I tell her, I'm betraying Jake. I promised him I wouldn't.' I put off ringing Patience until the afternoon to give my conscience a chance to settle.

She sounded serene at the end of the line. 'You'll be pleased with me, Eve. I've been sketching a lot, I may start painting again soon.'

'That's *marvellous*, Patience. Oh, I am glad.'

'I don't know why I've left it for so long.'

'Just an artistic blockage. We all get them, you know. You helped me get over my own, I couldn't have finished the novel without you organising the house. By the way it's much better here now, I think I may actually have tamed the ghosts. The parties seemed to have been successful.'

'How did it go last night? Did Jake turn up?'

'He did.' I could feel the blush beginning beneath my skin.

'Enjoy himself? Bet he did! Screwing some young slag in the passage.' Correction needed, from young to old, from passage to four-poster.

'He seemed to enjoy himself, yes.' Perfectly true, it had been a good night. Two bodies in tune with each other. It was possibly the first time that I had actually turned a friend into a lover. It was usually the other way around. But I didn't want to go on talking about Jake, I felt too uncomfortable with the topic.

'And how's Gareth?' The question brought a gloomy response.

'He's gone away. I won't be seeing him for a while. He writes though, quite a lot. They're rather good, his letters. It perks up the day, looking forward to the post.'

'Just as well you've started working again. Take your mind off men.'

'Gareth is the only man on my mind, the plural is

unnecessary. And how about you, what's cooking in that department? The usual stream, I expect. I've been thinking about you, Eve, lately. And I really do think that now you're more settled in yourself it might be time for you to start one stable friendship. A lover who is also a friend.'

Fifteen

It was uncanny, the timing of Patience's advice, for that
very same day Max and I were meeting for dinner. Our first
for eleven years. Max had been one of my three lovers, like
Lawrence, from all those years before Adam. I'd got Spring
to ring the number, pretending to be somebody's secretary.
Leaving my number for him to ring. When he rang, he
didn't know that it would be me at the end of the line. We
had to employ all this subterfuge because of his wife. It had
always been like that, and now that he was a Cabinet
Minister I didn't expect for one moment that the situation
would have changed. The constituents dictate the private
life of a politician, he is their chosen candidate and without
them there is no seat in Parliament. I had always understood that.

I'd tried not to think too much about seeing Max again,
not after having seen Lawrence in those early days after
Adam. But I was much stronger now, it was true, as
Patience had said. I was more settled in myself. It wasn't
important if things were as good between us as they used to
be. It would be enough just to resume the intimacy of warm
friendship.

He'd been round to the house twice already. Both times
we'd just talked and drank the champagne that he'd
brought. Lady Cynthia, his wife, would have been flattered
at how much of the conversation was centred on her and
her foibles, her driving ambition on Max's behalf, her coldness, her insensitivity towards their children, her extravag-
ances, the non-existence of their sex-life together. I listened
to it patiently, it had to be got out of the way, all this
domestic trivia. And while I was listening I just sat and
looked at the leonine head, the jut of the jaw, the splendid
set of the shoulders. He had always had the physique of an

athlete, Max. Strong, muscled legs, the easy, loping gait of a golfer. Not difficult to see why he ran away with the women's votes. And he was even more impressive to look at now than he had been before. More distinguished with his greying temples, the deepening lines on his face. Life had treated him, and his appearance, well. He was the embodiment of moral strength and decency, a family man, ideal husband material. No matter that in his own marriage this didn't apply. He looked the part, that was the important thing.

But there was a difference between us now, and how we used to be. The difference was me. Before, I had simply been a working journalist, my by-line was well known but I wasn't. Since then I had appeared frequently on television, other journalists had interviewed me and I had started writing novels. Now I was as much a celebrity as him. I could see that it might come between us.

We'd have to be doubly cautious for a start, seek out obscure restaurants where no-one we knew would dine. Where gossip-mongers from the media would never appear, places photographers wouldn't dream of patronising. Either that or I'd have to start cooking again myself, making meals for a man. It wasn't what I looked forward to. Why play the part of a wife when I was no longer one? The pampered mistress role was what I coveted now. We'd find a way of working it all out.

It was quite difficult trying to decide what to wear for our first dinner. I was somewhat short on discreet dresses that helped me fade into the background, mine now were all chosen for impact. Head-swivelling stuff. But I would have to do something about that, start adapting my wardrobe to my different men. I'd had to do it the last time I'd divorced, starting right from the bottom, having to replenish my supply of underwear. I didn't realise what a despairing state of disrepair I'd let my undies fall into. Having the same husband year in and year out can lead to sartorial negligence in the knicker and bra department, if you're not careful. You never imagine that they notice or care what you have on underneath. It was only the New York orgy scene which Adam and I had indulged in that galvanised me into buying seductive underwear (for us both). Now I must organise myself into getting some little ladylike dresses. The sort that the women around Marty's dinner table would be wearing. If only I could assume their impeccable manners at the same time. Some chance!

We held hands over dinner, our candlelit dinner, hardly taking our eyes off each other. Beneath the table our legs were entwined.

'It's wonderful being with you again, Eve.'

'Wonderful being with you too, Max – my darling.' I smiled at him, smothering my yawn. I was tired and above all I wanted to go to bed. I hadn't had much sleep with Jake the night before. But there were hours and hours ahead of me, I knew that. Max wanted to make the most of my company, he'd have to go home at some point, it wasn't possible for him to stay the night. After our fuck he'd light up a cigarette and want to talk some more. He had a passion for words, that's why he'd been drawn to politics. The spotlit platform was made for spouting. I had a sneaking suspicion that I might begin to find Max more than a little bit boring.

We were back in bed by one-thirty, a brief and unsatisfactory screw after which Max fell asleep, snoring. I was the one who lit up a cigarette, I wasn't sufficiently relaxed to be able to fall asleep. Had he been as bad a lover as this all those years ago? I could barely remember. But perhaps I was being too brutal. We were both probably as much of a disappointment to each other, through tiredness. We'd try again tomorrow, he'd asked me to dinner. Every dog deserves a second chance. Dear Max, he'd even talked about buying us a house, a love-nest, a pied-à-terre. Somewhere that I could furnish to my own taste. We could go together to Peter Jones for carpets and curtains, we could drive out to the country and scour the antique shops. We could even give small dinner-parties for the more discreet of our friends. Perhaps a romantic weekend in Paris might be arranged in the not too distant future. We were back together again. This was the important thing.

Smoking my post-coital cigarette I struggled to rationalise my sinking spirits. Depression was settling like a suffocating blanket around my shoulders. Max turned restlessly in his sleep, stretching towards me. His snoring stopped now that he was lying on his side. I looked at the top of his head and fondled it with my free hand. The scalp glimmered through the thinning strands of his hair. He probably minded very much about his incipient baldness, most men did. Adam especially, he used to lower his head like a charging bull and demand that I examine him for any signs of baldness. Once I'd said as a joke that yes, indeed, there'd been an increasing fall-out of follicles since the last time I'd looked. He'd called me a bitch, and hadn't laughed. But that was because there were signs now of a definite recession on the front of the forehead. He never asked me about that, the exaggerated widow's peak that was taking shape. He didn't have to, he could see for himself in the mirror.

The reminder of Adam led me to concentrate my thoughts on him. It wouldn't be that long now before my decree nisi came through, and then the decree absolute. Our divorce would be over and done with. It had been relatively painless this time, compared to the last, though I'd used the same solicitor on both divorces. My visits to his office had been lighthearted, in fact, and I was looking forward to being officially free again. I called the solicitor by his first name and regarded him as a friend. It was the same with my bank manager, my accountant, and my doctor. I'd been with Bruce, my doctor, for almost twenty years. He'd seen me through the pregnancy and birth of Scarlett. He'd operated on my varicose veins, he'd (reluctantly) supplied me with slimming pills in the sixties when it seemed important to assume the proportions of a pubescent girl, he'd fitted me with a coil, and checked that coil every six months for cancer of the cervix. There was nothing that I couldn't discuss with him.

He was the one who'd tried to dissuade me from embarking upon my final pregnancy at thirty-nine, but we'd wanted that child. Adam and I. And we were upset when it miscarried in the fourth month. But looking back on that small tragedy I understood that it was probably all for the best. Bringing up a child on my own was not what I needed now. Nor, any longer, did I need Adam. Neither did Adam need me.

He was living with Monika, and soon they would be leaving for New York. He preferred it over there, he felt his work would go better. Sometimes, seeing him at parties, our hands would reach out for each other. And we'd stand, just holding on. The brimming tears barely controlled. There was no kissing any longer, no need for Scarlett to tear us apart. And lately we hadn't even felt the compulsion to touch. We'd wave from separate sides of the room, once I had left without even saying hello. And thought no further of it. I had almost reached the point where I could ring him on the telephone to ask his advice, as one would a friend. Even have lunch together, though dinner alone might be dangerous. I was too reckless with drink to risk that. If asked, I would have to declare that there were only four men in my life now. The irreplaceable professionals. Solicitor. Bank Manager. Accountant. And Doctor. Oh – and Dentist, making five. That's all any girl really needs to get her through life, it's what I kept on telling my daughters.

I didn't go to dinner with Max the following night. His wife had arranged for them to attend a diplomatic reception at the Iranian Embassy and then to go on to a function at the Dorchester, in aid of one of the numerous charities which she supported. He was disappointed, bitterly so, but if he had a chance he would drop in on me during the day. All the local shops were shut by the time he arrived, I hadn't dared venture out earlier in case I should miss him. We made hasty love, with his trousers hanging at half-mast. I laddered a new pair of tights, trying to get one leg out in a rush. But the chauffeured Bentley was waiting outside, there was no time even for him to swill down his dwindling dick under the tap. Just stuff it back in his Jermyn Street jockey pants and head for the door. I wondered what the whisking crinolines thought when they witnessed the yanking of the trouser-zip, as it whizzed past them down the stairwell.

The following two weeks we had many such meetings. But I didn't mind, I was busy too. My novel was finished, the proofs had been returned from the printers. I had recorded two television shows, one a celebrity quiz on the cinema of the fifties. Another, a lunatic mime game with a studio audience, which I managed marginally well but not as brilliantly as my fellow panellists. In addition I did a live midday television interview up in Manchester. And an early-morning disc-jockey radio show for one of the London commercial stations. Also I'd been commissioned to write an original screenplay, based on Henry VIII. I looked forward to that.

Looking back I couldn't imagine how I'd managed to fit in five of my other casual lovers, on top of all that. But considering the fact that straightforward fucking can be anything from a frenzied, five-minute fire-cracker to a flowing, twenty-four-hour flood-tide, I supposed that anything is possible if you want it. And whether I wanted it or not, it was there on the doorstep. My juices were flowing, my adrenalin was high, the wave-lengths were twanging. I really loved life . . .

And then the telephone call came.

'Eve, it's me. Jake. Not very good news, I'm afraid. I waited until I was sure that what I suspected was true and now it's been confirmed. A case of the clap. I've got gonorrhoea. I do suggest that you have a check-up, darling.'

'Shit!'

'Yes, it is a little bit shitty. Sorry, my sweet!' He sounded as sunny as ever.' But it's only a social disease, clears up in no time. Couple of days off the booze, keep taking the tablets. Well, you know, you've probably been through this before.'

'No, I haven't. I've never caught it, not all that time in New York. . . .' I felt nauseous. I had to sit down, but felt cautious about contaminating the cushion on the chair. I removed it and sat on the polished oak surface. Tainted I may be, but it wasn't with wood-worm. The chair was presumably immune to the pestilent pox. Jake's cheerful voice reached me.

'Well, you're probably one of those fortunate people who are immune to such diseases. Best to tell you though, just in case. I always tell people. After this call I have to put in several others. They aren't going to be too pleased with me either!'

'God in heaven!' I'd just thought of Max – and of the others. They would have to be told. 'I'm just totting up the ones I'll have to tell, at least one of them is going to be appalled.'

'It's just the initial shock, then they get over it, you'll find. But you have to let them know, it's only self-protection because if you go to bed with them again after you've had the cure, they may re-infect you. You see what I mean?'

'Where do you think you caught yours, Jake?'

'Difficult to work out, but it might well have been a stripper I'd had the night before you. On the other hand it could have been the sexy feminist on your bathroom floor.'

'Or me, Jake.' I said it slowly. This was the first time that this had happened to me, but there was a first time for everything. And I had been pretty hectic in bed since Adam, more like Paddington Station than a lady's boudoir.

'Well, have any of your other gentlemen callers put in a complaint yet?' They hadn't, but if I'd caught anything from Jake they should start suspecting something soon.

'Where will I go for my check-up, Jake?'

'You can go privately to your doctor or, as I do, to the VD clinic in your nearest hospital.'

'But doesn't everybody recognise you?' I was fearful and appalled.

'Yes, it's rather jolly, I've been going there for years. I make a point of having a check-up every so often anyway. Just to be on the safe side. You should think of doing the same, Eve, now that you're leading the normal sex life of a single girl.' He laughed.

'You may well laugh, Jake. Neither your sex-life, nor mine, would ever be considered normal.'

'All the more reason to be sensible.'

'Pretty good reason to give it up. I've never tried the life in a nunnery.'

'You wouldn't like it there, Eve. Wax candles don't work, not the same satisfaction. Besides, the wick tickles. I've tried them, to copious complaints.'

160

The telephone rang just as I'd found Bruce's number in my phone book. The surgery would still be open if I got a move-on, he could take a blood sample tonight. It must have been auto-suggestion. Until Jake's call I'd felt in tip-top condition, sleakly healthy like a well-cared-for cat. Now I felt like a diseased rat. Which is what I was.

'Eve? Thank God you're in. I'm in a terrible state! Jake's told me he's given me VD. I've started on the tablets already, before it's even confirmed. I had to go to my gynaecologist to have a blood sample taken, but it takes twenty-four hours for the results to come through, and I haven't the time. Gareth is coming back in ten days' time, possibly sooner and if I haven't taken the full treatment by then I shan't be clear – and I'll give him gonorrhoea. It will be the end between us if he finds out that I've slept with anyone else, especially with my husband. He's passion-ately jealous, he'd beat me black and blue, I know it. Can you imagine – the first time in ten years that I let Jake into my bed and this is what he gives me. I can't even bear to look at him!'

'I'm speechless . . .' I said weakly. 'I don't know what to say.' I did know. I could say, I understand how you feel, kid. The same blow has just been delivered my way, not five minutes ago. I've been dumped with a dose, we're the same team. But the anguished voice was continuing.

'It happened the night that I came back to London, about five days after your party. Jake took me to Langan's for dinner – well, you remember, we saw you there as you were leaving. We should have left too, then I wouldn't have got so drunk. By the time we got home it was about two in the morning. I was feeling rather affectionate towards Jake by then. I'd shown him all my sketches and told him my idea for this big painting. I thought, Eve's right, I should be nicer to him. He's a marvellous man really. So one thing led to another and I let him into my bed. The bastard. He thinks he caught it from a *stripper* – can you imagine anyone going to bed with a stripper and not considering that they may catch the clap! And then to go to bed with their wife after that! Well, I've told him that I shall never, ever go to bed with him again. He's walking around now with a wounded

161

expression on his face as if *he's* the wronged one . . .'

By the time Patience had finished the fiendishly ironic tale of woe, Bruce's clinic was closed. And would now be closed until Monday morning. My disease would have these further few days of the festering weekend to rampage through my contaminated carcass.

Sixteen

Spring and Scarlett were quite sanguine over the whole affair. Not to say jocular.

'We'd better steer clear of Mum's bathroom and stick with our own, Spring.' Scarlett nudged her sister. 'Not very nice, catching the pox from a parent. We could report you to the RSPCC.'

'Poor old disease-riddled Mumples. Has the end of your nose dropped off yet?'

'Don't joke,' I said feebly. I was feeling terribly ill, I didn't expect to make it through to Monday. I had gradually recalled conversations with friends over the years, who had contracted venereal disease. First the throat starts aching, then the head starts pounding, then the private parts start pumping like oil gushing from an oil-well (best get Castrol in as a consultant), then it starts stinging when you take a piss, then, then . . .

'I've got all these symptoms, girls.' I described everything to them. They'd both shrugged. So, big deal? The pox was nothing, they had pals who'd had it, sometimes six or seven times. An occupational hazard of having a good time. I'd be over it in no time. Nice and clean, my slate would be – to start all over again. They were sweet children, trying to be kind and offer me comfort. It didn't ease my state of mind at all. Nor did the telephone talks with Patience. Those were the worse because I wanted to give her all my support in her mental agony. If we had ever shared anything in the past we should be sharing this now. I needed her as a friend as much as she needed me, to be able to laugh it all off. And I would have made a joke of it, if I'd been able to tell her that I'd been to bed with Jake. I'd even rung him on his separate line to beg to be able to tell her. But he was firm. He said that it would make matters worse between them than it even was at the moment. And I could very well see that it might, so I kept quiet. I couldn't wait for Monday morning to come.

'What I can't understand, Eve, is why you're still bashing away at it at your age.' I was the first patient in the surgery.

'Bruce, be a good boy and just get on with things. I'm lying here naked from the navel downwards and you start giving me a lecture. It's not what I need.'

'Perhaps it's exactly what you do need. The horizontal position is obviously the one that comes easiest to you. How better to capture your attention?'

'OK. You suggest that I give up sex altogether?'

'Some selectivity would probably be a good start. Had you considered that?' He was rummaging around my inside like a daily with a duster.

'Christ, Bruce! This isn't meant to be a hysterectomy, you're not unplugging the whole thing to force me to a life of celibacy, are you?'

He laughed, throwing back his head. 'I give up on you, Eve. But I applaud your spirit. How's the work going, still writing?'

'What is that supposed to mean – still writing? What would I live on if I weren't still writing? I don't ask you if you're still practising – though I might well this morning. Still practising, not yet skilled at the job. You can be awfully clumsy with a person's cunt, Bruce.'

He slapped me lightly. 'Yours is up to it, old girl. Now, up with your rump and get dressed. I'll get this off today, together with your blood test. And I'll let you know the worst tomorrow, when the report comes back from the lab. I trust you'll behave youself between now and then. You never know, you might be completely clear, but could catch something from an entirely different source tonight.'

'I'm staying in, and looking at the telly. But I'll bandage my eyes when a pair of trousers appears on the screen. How's that for abstinence?'

'Ridiculously exaggerated – as one would expect from you, Eve. There is such a thing as learning to grow old gracefully.' I blew him a crude raspberry in reply.

I hung around the telephone the whole of the next day. It

had been difficult, putting Max off. I'd had to tell him that I was working with the film producer who'd commissioned the screenplay. And this was true, she had come over to discuss ideas, which helped to take my mind off Bruce's news. I was convinced now that the results would be positive, that I was definitely down with the pox. Though Patience had rung to say that hers had been negative, so far. There was was another wait of twenty-four hours to be on the safe side. She too was convinced that she definitely had it, despite the negative result. She said she just *knew*, never mind what the experts said. She felt unclean from her toenails to the top of her head.

'You can't begin to imagine the feeling, because you're not going through this, Eve. If you were you'd be able to understand.' I was silent, biting my tongue. Longing to tell. She misconstrued my silence.

'You would probably agree with Jake and think that I'm over-dramatising the whole thing. You wouldn't blame him if you were me, and just accept it as bad luck. But I can't. I do blame him. He claims it to be no more important than a common cold, but I don't. I think of it as the putrid result of thoughtless promiscuity.'

'Yes, well . . .' I trailed off, uncertain of what to say. I didn't blame Jake for the position I found myself in now. After all, our coupling was a fifty-fifty decision. I thought it was hard luck on poor Patience, certainly. But I also did think that it was sad for Jake. To have waited ten years for the woman he loved more than anything in the world – and then for this to have happened. If they'd gone to bed together, even a fortnight earlier than they did, everything would be different: their marriage, their life together, their future. As it was, it had created a bitterness in Patience that hadn't been there before. And I didn't want to add to that.

'Eve?' It was Bruce. 'You must have some fairy godmother looking after you. Or the luck of the devil. The results have come through and it seems to be favourable.' He laughed. 'I expect you'll go out now and celebrate, knowing you. But don't go overboard until tomorrow, there's a good girl. It won't be absolutely one hundred per cent certain until then.'

Of course I went out. I went to a party and took Scarlett, but I rang Spring first at the theatre to tell her. And I picked up the telephone to tell Patience, only just realising in time that it wasn't allowed, I couldn't do it. It was just that I was longing to tell somebody. The relief of it was so overwhelming.

Adam was the first person I saw at the party. So Adam was the one I told. And Adam was the one who told Patience.

I should have guessed that he might from his attitude the next day on the telephone. He rang me just after Bruce's call with the latest results of my test. *Bad news this time.* I'd have to come in for the prescription. Bruce had been affably sympathetic.

'*Cest la vie*, Bruce!' It was only what I had expected. The hopeful news of yesterday had been merely a temporary reprieve.

So when Adam had rung moments after, I'd told him this latest development too, unprepared for the reproof that followed. He felt that I was being deeply disloyal to his old friend Patience, by telling everybody that I'd been to bed with Jake behind her back.

'Who's everybody?' I was astonished at the coldness of his tone. I knew that he and Patience still went swimming together and it was true that he'd known her for much longer than I had, as he'd known Jake. So in a sense he could claim them as his friends and not mine, but that didn't mean to say that I now had to cut them out of my life. Or that I was banned from going to bed with one of them. 'Who's everybody, Adam?' I repeated the question, parrot-fashion, to give myself some form of defence. Hadn't I told him just how bad I felt about Patience, surely he'd understood that. 'The only people who know are the girls and yourself. And Jake, of course, I shouldn't think that Jake has forgotten.'

'That's what I mean, your flippant attitude to it all. Poor Patience, she probably thinks of you as a friend.'

I didn't answer. He had his own motivations for this attack. Like jealousy, for instance. I'd only just thought of that. He admired Jake immensely, always had. He probably would have liked to have been to bed with Jake, himself. On the other hand he might still feel jealousy over me. That was another possibility.

Patience rang me that afternoon, just after I'd returned from the chemist and was taking my first pill.

'I know, Eve.' She said it quietly. The world stopped turning. 'Adam told me. I've just got back from our swim.'

'I'm so sorry, Patience.' It's all I could think of to say. The words sounded futile and insincere, and indescribably hollow in my ears.

'I don't mind about you going to bed with Jake. I'm not talking about that. I mean I know about your latest results, you must be feeling absolutely rotten. I wish you'd told me yourself, we could have commiserated with each other all over the ghastly weekend. I could have done with you sitting here. I had to drink all on my own, sitting up in bed. Yes, I know you're not meant to drink whilst you're taking the bloody pills, but all it does is lessen their effectiveness slightly. And if I hadn't drunk I would have gone completely round the twist. Do you want to come over now, we can hold each other's hands.'

'I can't,' I said dully. 'I've got Max coming in a minute. I've got to break the bad news to him in a minute. Stone cold sober, it's not going to be easy. And then to five others, it's a fabulous way to spend an evening. I'll ring you later, Patience. You're lovely, taking it this way, you know. I've felt absolute dross about the whole thing, ever since it happened. Having to be dishonest with you, of all pals. But I *hate* you having learned of it through Adam.'

She laughed. 'Don't blame Adam, he thought he was doing it for the best. He knew I was worried about Gareth's reaction, that he might beat me up and was warning me that what had happened with your test could happen with mine. That the final result may after all be positive. For some reason mine seems to be taking longer than yours in coming through.'

'Yes,' I pointed out, 'but you started taking the pills five days sooner than me, so you must be almost clear by now, even supposing you ever got gonorrhoea.'

'Oh, don't even say the word, Eve! Gonorrhoea! It's so

167

ugly, the ugliest word I've ever heard. Such an apt description for the condition. By the way – did you ever get any symptoms?'

'Actually, no. If Jake hadn't told me, I would never have known. Though the minute he did, I imagined everything was happening. The whole thing rotting and suppurating and stinking, it felt awful. But now that I've taken my first pill I feel better already. Susceptible to suggestion, that's what it is.'

'I'm just the same,' Patience sighed.

'I tell you another reason I feel better too, knowing that you know about Jake and me. That made me feel worse, I think, than the social disease. I've never thought that a fuck is worth forfeiting a female friendship for, but my mind had departed my body that night. The flesh was weak, you know what I mean?'

'I do indeed. My flesh was weak with Jake the other night too.' I thought that she sounded sweetly wistful.

Max was marvellous. I could hardly believe the matter-of-fact way in which he accepted what I told him.

'Better get along to my medical man tomorrow, no problem. Do me good to cut down on the old booze anyway. A few days off it and I'll be able to concentrate on these documents that have piled up of late.' I was amazed, it made me think that this wasn't his first time. And there was obviously no concern over having passed it onto his wife. If I'd ever needed proof that he wasn't screwing her, this surely was it.

But of course I had told him that I must have contracted the disease several days before he, himself, had come back on the scene. I didn't think he'd take kindly to me telling him that it was actually after. Or that when he'd gone I now had to ring five others to tell them.

The younger ones were the most put out. That surprised me at first, I would have thought that they'd take Spring and Scarlett's attitude and make flip jokes about it. But one said, 'Jesus, what a bummer!' And both the others couldn't believe that I would have been with anybody else apart from them. Though one of those admitted he had himself. 'This is going to make it bloody difficult for someone. She's

168

married,' he said. 'Her old man's going to go up the fucking wall!'

The two older ones took it philosophically, as Max had done. They were men of the world. A VD clinic held no terrors for them. One asked whether it was syphilis or gonorrhoea. The other wanted to know if I had genital herpes. 'They are the real killer to get rid of – a raging epidemic in the States, and getting to be the same over here.' I was learning a lot this evening.

Before leaving, since we could neither drink nor make love, Max took me on a walk around the streets of Chelsea. He wanted to point out a couple of houses which had caught his attention as he'd passed by in the Bentley. Ones which he thought might meet with my approval, quite close to Cheyne Walk. We strolled the darkened pavements arm in arm like devoted old-age pensioners. I thought to myself, he's planning his future retirement from politics, a future which he obviously wants to spend with me. The depression settled on me again.

It remained with me long after he'd left me, to go back for one of his children's birthday parties. A dance for young adults held in the wife's ancestral home. I could imagine the affair, the sort of smart shindig that I'd attended in my first marriage. Green lawns ringing with asinine guffaws and high-pitched whinnyings, girls in pastel ballgowns puking up amongst the peonies. Gout-suffering old aristocrats passing the port and rambling over their reminiscences, all with raspberry-red snouts spreading into their cheeks. Max wished that I could come too.

'Mm, be lovely,' I'd murmured. I couldn't wait to get back into the isolated comfort of the house when the Bentley had gone.

'I'm back,' I shouted around. The once terrifying shadows engulfed me as I carried my depression up the stairs. I stopped outside the ghoulish floor and, on impulse, I went in and switched on the crystal ball. Then I sat on the window-sill smoking a cigarette, trying to imagine what happenings these four walls had witnessed. Just watching the snowflakes of light drifting around. Completely in harmony with the house, each of us appreciating the presence of the other.

Both the girls were out. It was Spring's night off from the theatre and she was going out with Joe, which meant that she would be sleeping at his place. Scarlett was staying down in her friends' cottage, there was a party at the art school. I would be alone all night in the house. But that didn't worry me now, in a strange way I enjoyed it. Cocooned in the womb, with my ghosts watching over me, and the carved gargoyles and angels of the four-poster shielding me from danger as I slept.

I sat in the bed and watched television until the end of transmission. Then I took another pill, turned off all the lights and went to sleep. The time on my alarm clock said eleven-fifty. It was the last thing I saw.

The next thing I saw were the figures of two men in the room, one of them lurching towards my bed. I sat up, instantly awake. I was frozen with fear, hardly capable of speech, yet completely in control of my faculties. Like a trapped animal, I could have fought these intruders, or run like a hare. But I sat, rigid, waiting for them to make the first move.

I thought of the front door. I knew that I had locked it as securely as I always had done. To my certain knowledge these two men couldn't have gained entry any other way but through that door. Every window or outside door was impossibly difficult to force. Unless these were professional burglars and knew of other ways and means. After all, there had been all those burglaries the year before this.

But the lights were shining through into the room from the landing outside. Surely burglars wouldn't switch lights on in a house they planned to burgle. Didn't they traditionally work with torches? These panicking thoughts were whirling through my head when one of them spoke.

'Hello, doll-face. It's Terence, old Terry is back from his wanderings. C'mon, give us a kiss to welcome me back!' He staggered onto the bed, reeking of alcohol. His companion came forward to stop him falling to the floor.

'Hey, Terry. Hold on, old chap. We've given the little lady a fright. Sorry . . .' He looked at me. I'd turned on the bedside light, noting that now it was three-thirty in the morning. 'I did say to old Terry here that this would be a bad idea. But our yacht only just docked tonight. He's had a skinful as you can see, but all he's talked about is you on this last trip. He's told everyone in the club tonight that you two are going to get married. He insisted on coming round . . .' The companion's voice fell away. He could see the rage in my face. I exploded.

'What the fuck do you think you're doing, Terry!!! You burst in here blind, bloody drunk at three-thirty in the morning – how dare you! Just piss off out of it!! I mean it . . .'

'I adore you, my l'il' precious. She gonna be my wife. We're getting married . . .' he said thickly to his companion. My eyes flickered witheringly over to his companion.

'How did you get in here, anyway? I demand to know. Immediately!'

He looked frightened and abashed in the face of my obvious wrath. 'We . . . old Terry had a key . . .' I spun round on the slobbering drunkard.

'I stole your key, when I was here before. That time we met.'

'Give it to me! This instant.' I raised my fist towards his face. He placed the key on the bed with a shaking hand. 'Thank you very much. Now just get out of here before I call the police!'

The companion was backing nervously. 'I'll leave you two lovers to work it out between you.' Then he turned around and had disappeared downstairs on his own, leaving the sodden Terry for me to cope with as best I could.

'Terry, I'm warning you – follow your friend now, or else!' But it was no use, I knew, he was no lightweight, this one. And Irish, stubborn. I'd had trouble shaking him off the first time I'd met him at the opening of a club owned by John Conteh, the boxer. That was before he'd cruised away on his yacht. I never did discover who he made his money, for there was plenty of that. The Rolls Royce. The Mayfair mews. The wallet crammed with cash. The ostentatious, jewelled cufflinks, the gold watch. The girls had referred to him as my gangster and treated him as a joke, though he'd only been around twice, the second time without an invita-

171

tion. Like now. I'd be damned if I'd let him stay. Revolting slob. He was sprawled right across my bed now, refusing to move.

'Right – I'm calling the police, Terry,' I said. He laughed appreciatively, enjoying the joke, not believing for a minute. When he saw me dial, he simply stared, then shut his eyes and pretended to feign sleep. The police said they'd be around within five minutes. And they were, three of them. It needed that number to control Terry. He fought them, all three, like a cornered rat. But when they eventually overpowered him he sank to his knees, like Samson. I was Delilah, I'd betrayed him.

'Why, d'you do this to me, doll-face?' He pleaded with me, brokenly. But I stared resolutely the other way.

'Come on now, sir. The lady would like you out of the house.' One of the policemen guided him through the front door. He refused to leave the step.

'No, sir. That is out of the house but it is not off the premises. We require you to step out into the street.' They had to drag him again, he'd started bellowing now.

'I demand to know your number, officer. And I would like my lawyer to be present here . . .'

'Christ,' I groaned.' He's going to wake up the whole of Cheyne Walk.'

'No,' reassured the youngest-looking policeman. 'We'll see to it that he goes quietly now. Do you think he may try and come back?'

'Well, you can see the state he's in. There's no knowing what he'll do. I tell you I am a bit nervous, I'm in the house all on my own.'

'If he tries anything, don't hesitate to ring the station again.' I went back upstairs with foreboding. I didn't feel that I'd seen the last of Terry by any means.

And I was right. No sooner had the police car driven off (why in hell hadn't they taken him with them?) than Terry started staggering back up the garden path. I could see it all from my bedroom window. I stood watching there, with the lights off.

'Fucking bastard!' I swore as I telephoned the station a second time. Terry was downstairs, kicking at the front door, his finger pressed continuously on the bell. It pealed throughout the house. He was obviously going to fuse it. He was still on it when the police arrived. This time, with an even greater struggle than the last time, they forced him out to the street and into the car with them. Now he'd probably be charged with being drunk and disorderly, making a nuisance of himself. His own fault, not mine.

Yet as I lay in bed, unable to sleep at all now, alert to every sound in the creaking house, I wondered. This wasn't the first time this had happened. I'd had to call the police once before to a beswotted swain who'd persistently tried to break into where I was living. They had led him away crying. He'd had to spend the entire night in a cell before being charged and fined in the morning. And that still hadn't deterred him. He continued to press his unwelcome attentions upon me. Perhaps there was something in me that provoked such lunatic love. The inability to say no, the grasping at every human encounter as if it may be the last and therefore must be made as much of as possible. It led people to expect more from me than I was capable of giving so that in an effort of desperation they offered themselves utterly, and in the end abjectly, in order to evoke the same commitment from me. Which meant that in the ultimate reckoning of any relationship I was taking more and giving less, when what I'd intended was exactly the opposite. I fell asleep troubled, resolving to remould myself on more generous lines, become less self-occupied, less detached, more genuinely caring. Yet knowing that like all repenters, whatever my resolves, I would continue to cause emotional chaos around me and pursue my own selfish path, unaffected. Patience was right, I was like Jake. Promiscuity was our natural ambience, except that Jake was elevated by his love for her. I loved nobody more than myself, only my mother and my children.

Seventeen

'I suppose you'll be out on the piss, picking up pieces of rubbish now that your purified again, eh, Mum?'

'Actually, Scarlett, I shall be staying at home. I've relinquished the life of debauchery.'

'Glad to hear it, Mumples. Would you think about cooking me a meal for when I get back from the theatre.'

'What would you like?'

'Cauliflower cheese, please. And could you take my washing to the launderette, and if you've got time would you iron that white dress for me. The one with all the frills, it takes me forever.'

'Anything else?' I'd intended heavy irony but Spring had chosen to ignore that.

'If I think of anything I'l give you a ring from the theatre. Thanks, Mumples. It's nice to think of you being a Mummy again, instead of sexual competition.'

'I don't think I agree with this situation you're forcing her into. Domestic drudgery isn't the answer, Spring. Why don't you just go round all the galleries, Mum? You never do that any more.'

'I did enough of it for ten years, when I was a painter, certainly when I was a student, like you. And when I was with Adam. Now I'm more interested in the written word, and the spoken word. I might start going to the theatre more.'

'On your own?' Spring looked astonished. 'You never go anywhere on your own, Mumples.'

'True. But I don't know why not.'

'"We are each of us an island." Who said that, Mum?' Scarlett looked at me thoughtfully. I didn't know the answer, I wasn't even certain that she was quoting it correctly.

'I leave you to enlighten me, darling.' I smiled sweetly,

passing the buck.

'I'm rather looking forward to my new life, actually. The fresh start I should have made when I split up with Adam, instead of hurling myself into all this meaningless sexual activity.' Both girls nodded vigorously.

'Well, you've got it out of your system now – by the way, Mumples, I meant to ask. Did that good-looking druggie manage to get it up with you, because that's where I slept last night after the party. He was hopeless, nothing, a dead loss. Rather a pity, I always fancied him when he used to come around after you. Perhaps it was my youth and inexperience, I didn't turn him on.'

'Don't worry, I didn't either. He was completely impotent, shame. Too much smack, you'd have got him going if he wasn't on that.'

'That's OK then. I was beginning to get worried that your sex appeal might be more potent than mine!'

'Sister – stop all this sex talk. Our mother has just announced that she's given it up. You mustn't whet her appetite again, that's not the right encouragement for an addict. We must help her as much as we can.'

As it happened they were neither of them, Spring or Scarlett, prevailed upon to help me. I had to leave London, I had to leave all temptation behind for the higher call of duty. I had to go down to Wales to stay with my mother. Fate had interfered on my behalf.

My sister was going away with my brother-in-law, and my niece was on a camping holiday in Brittany. Someone would be needed to be close to my mother, who was now too frail to look after herself properly. She could still move around, but with immense difficulty. She could still fill the electric kettle with water and switch it on to boil, but there was a fear that she might have an accident in the home. My sister popped in more than once every day, depending on how my mother was. Sometimes she was less confused than usual, other times she was more. I was going to stay down there, actually sleep in her house, for something like a month.

'Well, there are certainly no men down there who I might fancy, so I should be all right.'

175

'Do you want to bet? In hard cash, I mean.' Scarlett was rather short of money.

'Well, I'll bet that by the end of a month I will not have gotten laid – is that the right expression?'

'It is and I do – bet you. Ten pounds, done.'

The girls helped me pack, though I was taking hardly anything. I needed their advice on what exactly to take. The end result was a mish-mash of my Oxfam and their old ordinaire. Nothing startling, nothing highly glamorous, everything comfortable enough to trudge over the pebbled beaches. Wellington boots for the rain. Only one hat allowed, and that was one that I'd knitted myself one cold winter in Devon. I didn't know what the weather was like for this coming month. I just needed this pull-on cap to hide my hair. Whilst I was down there I intended going back to my natural hair-colour – a grown-up grey. But I didn't tell anyone that, not even the girls. It was meant to be a pleasant surprise to show how serious I really was about this ageing gracefully and giving up sex.

Before I went I had lunch alone with Adam. He was flying to the States the next day.

I was early, he was precisely on time. While I waited for him I had a chance to survey the restaurant. It had changed since we used to come here in those tempestuous first months of our falling in love. Though the management remained the same and the staff greeted me with affectionate Italian effusion, as they always had in the past, the clientèle had moved on, including ourselves, to more fashionable venues. I only recognised one person. At another time the faces at every table would have been familiar. This girl had been a model in the fifties, that far back, whilst I was stuck at home with the children, painting my portraits and landscapes, but mostly just waiting for Henry to come home. Her husband had been at Oxford with Henry, for a brief time they had even worked for the same firm. So that we'd meet at the firm's various social functions, dutifully playing our parts as decorative wives (she being infinitely more alluring than me). And we'd complain of the boredom together in the ladies' cloakroom, whilst we back-combed our lacquered beehives, and re-applied our pearly-white lipsticks. She looked altogether different now, as I did. But I hadn't seen or heard of her for almost twenty years.

'Eve, darling – how are you? You look *stunning!*' I struggled to remember her name, it must have shown on my face.

'Vanessa.' She laughed and grimaced. 'I know I've aged, but surely not that much!'

'Quite the contrary – I couldn't for the life of me place who this youthful vision of loveliness was. You look younger now than you did twenty years ago. Honestly.' It was true. Her jaw-line was creaseless and clear from ear-lobe to chin. There was not even a suggestion of one laughter-line (euphemism for wrinkle) either around her eyes or her mouth. The face was that of a porcelain china doll, unreal in its flawless perfection. She leaned forward, I caught the musk of her perfume, the diamond flash of her earrings, the shampooed gloss of her expensively cut hair. She reminded me of New York, where every career woman looked like this. Ageless, anything from twenty-three to thirty-eight.

'Well, Eve, I must say,' she was whispering in my ear, 'I am rather pleased myself. I've had it all done again this year. If you ever need someone sensational for your first lift you must go to this surgeon, he's the tops. Here's my card, give me a ring soon and we can have a hen-party. I'll get some of my girlfriends over so you can see what this guy had done for their faces.' I watched her walking away, the six-foot slenderness of the former model was still there, the greyhound legs, the boyish buttocks. She'd probably had those taken up too, the buttocks. These girls were always manically preoccupied with the drop of their buttocks, once those had gone it meant the cancellation of all swimwear work, mini-shorts, nude shots. And they could drop no matter how slim the girl managed to stay. I had always thanked Fate that in my past profession as a fashion editor, I was able to crouch the right side of the camera, not having to depend on swell and sag for my livelihood. There must be a streak of masochism required of all models if they are to be successful.

I looked at the man she'd gone to rejoin, his eyes flickered in my direction then dropped with disinterest. We didn't like each other at all. It was chalk and cheese. Nobody who would ever be with Vanessa, looking as she did, could possibly be attracted to me. I studied the card she'd given me but saw that her name wasn't on it, only his. For I recognised him now as the son of a construction firm tycoon. Vanessa must be living with this millionaire builder, reconstructing her own personal building site every year to keep the façade fresh and modern.

Adam walked in, or rather he sauntered in, wearing a new suit. I noticed that right away because it wasn't one that I had chosen for him. A small stabbing pain, but only a tremor. And I saw that his hair was a shade lighter today. He'd just been to the hairdresser to have it done, ready for his trip.

He saw me right away and kept his eyes on mine until he'd reached my chair. Then he bent to kiss me on both cheeks, like a friendly acquaintance. When we'd met here in the early days he'd nearly knock the other tables over to get to me, and I would rise and rush to meet him, if I'd arrived first. Which wasn't very often then. Marriage to Adam had at least taught me the importance of punctuality. Then we'd kiss, full on the lips, with all the restaurant looking on. Perhaps this wasn't such a good place to choose after all, I don't think I would have suggested it. There were too many nostalgic memories.

'I thought it would be a good idea to eat here, on nostalgic grounds.' He smiled easily, then leaned forward. 'Good to see you, you're looking *great*.'

'So are you. Very boyish. Lovely suit, I always thought that grey flannel would look nice on you.'

'I think that's what made me get it, remembering that you'd said that.' Small silence.

'How's the work going?'

'The work's going fine. I'm doing a new print. How's your work coming along?'

'Coming along slowly, but it will be all right. Just that I'm doing a screenplay as opposed to a novel. There's a difference with trying to write the whole thing in dialogue.'

'You're very good at dialogue. I always said you should do a screenplay.'

'Perhaps that's why I'm doing it, remembering that you'd said that.'

We both laughed. From then on, it was easy-going. Easier than I could have imagined it would be. We talked about Patience and Jake. He was going swimming with Patience later on that afternoon, giving a chance for this meal to settle first. I told him I'd given up the daily swim. He was drinking Perrier, whilst I had white wine. He was not smoking, whilst I was. The differences were widening between us.

'What about you and Jake? Is that still going on?'

'We're still friends, but I don't think we'll go to bed together again.'

'What about you and Monika? Are you in love with her?'

He didn't answer, just looked at his plate. Then he spoke without lifting his eyes.

'I'm not like you, Eve. I have to be with somebody. I can't be on my own, I never have been.'

I reached over and touched his hand. 'I know. You don't have to tell me.'

He drove me home in the borrowed car of the friends that he was staying with. As I got into it he apologised.

'A simple saloon car. Hardly your taste, Eve. Sorry.'

I smiled, there was no need to say anything. When we arrived at Cheyne Walk, I didn't ask him in. We just sat in the front of the car, both staring straight ahead. The moment of parting had come. The final goodbye. There was no knowing when he would be back from the States, or if we would ever see each other again.

He turned to me at the exact moment of me turning to him. Our arms wound compulsively around each other's necks, our closed mouths met, dry lips on dry. Neither daring to allow sensuality to enter the embrace. I silently left the car without even saying goodbye.

The following evening I had dinner with Patience and Jake. I was on television in a book programme around eight, and Jake was on the opposite channel, three-quarters of an hour later. We neither of us cared to view ourselves, preferring to sit around the kitchen table watching Patience preparing the food. She took a long time and great care over everything and would only allow us to help with the simplest tasks, like shelling peas or peeling potatoes. As if we were children, pleasingly willing but clumsily incompetent. We basked contentedly in her glow, drinking her home-made elderberry wine, salivating at the succulant odours emanating from the oven, anticipating the deliciousness of the meal she would put before us. And discussing plans for a gallery exhibition of her paintings.

I'd been staggered by how much work she was producing, but was as much impressed by the transformation in herself. She had returned to an earlier identity. It wasn't because of what she was wearing, an ancient dressing gown of Jake's dating back to his schooldays. Or that she was barefoot and devoid of all make-up. It wasn't the short, startlingly spiky haircut, or the stunning suntan. It was to do with an internal change, a shifting of the mind. When she spoke of each various sketch as we sifted through the sheets of paper, it was with such fervour that we fell silent, Jake and I. Her passion placed her beyond us, yet we, of all her intimates, understood what the rediscovery of her talent represented. For so many years she had channelled her visual gift into her surroundings, into the rooms of the numerous homes she had created from empty houses. Into the clothes she had made for her children, into the fashionable images of herself which she'd chosen to present to the world and to the passing lovers in her life. But now she'd turned that same eye to the countryside which she loved and was depicting so lyrically onto her canvases. This was her latest and would be her lasting romance. Her need to be needed was no longer there. The inner strength was incandescent, so that her enhanced prettiness had become exquisite.

We ate fish for dinner and afterwards Jake did the washing-up, whilst Patience and I tested the egg-nog that we'd made together some months ago. It was so thick that we had to eat it with a spoon, and so seductively alcoholic that Jake had to dial for my taxi first before joining us for his share. We didn't think he'd manage it after. I wouldn't be seeing them for a month, but there was always the telephone. We'd be in constant touch as usual.

Waving from the withdrawing taxi to both of them standing, framed, in the doorway, I thought what a marvellously mellow evening it had been. And how our shared disease had brought the three of us so much closer together. Maybe that's why it is known as the social disease instead of anti-social, as one would expect.

I travelled down to my mother's on a Sunday, since Spring and Scarlett wanted to wave me off from the station and it was the one certain day of the week on which they were both free at the same time. We had lunch at Foxtrot Oscar, a tiny and newly opened, but already fashionable restaurant, along the road from Cheyne Walk.

The two Michaels and Rex, the three partners, were in today. They hailed us jovially, we'd become regulars there from the start, mainly because of its nearness but mostly because of the intimate atmosphere and the fact that these three we now looked upon as pals. In fact Foxtrot Oscar, Langan's Brasserie, the Chelsea Arts Club, and the Zanzibar Club in Covent Garden were really the only places in which we did eat. The only spots where escorts usually took us, and where we always knew that we'd bump into friends. Which is the main enjoyment in eating out.

'Hello, girls. Hello, Spring. Hello, Scarlett. Hello, Eve.'

'Hello, Michael. Hello, Rex. Hello, Michael.'

'What, girls – no escorts today?'

'No escorts. Today, boys, we've dispensed with all males.'

'Even us?'

'We allow you to sit with us for one minute, no longer. We have female matters to discuss.'

What we were actually discussing was our holiday. In August, which was when Spring would have two weeks' holiday from the theatre, we were thinking of going to Venice. Neither of the girls had ever been to Venice, and I felt that their education was sadly lacking. Together with New York, I had always found it to be the most visually breathtaking place in the world. And the fact that both of these cities were man-made creations transformed them in my view into even more of a marvel. Architecture: an urban sprawl, a geodesic dome, a pre-fabricated hut, have always excited me more than a forest or a field of grass. I wanted to show off Venice to Spring and Scarlett, but first I wished to discuss it over a bottle of champagne. I wouldn't be in a position to buy them lunch for a month, after all. And I was now finally finding my own feet financially.

'Champagne, I think, girls – what do you say?' A chorus of agreement. We tilted our glasses and toasted each other.

'To our holiday in Venice!' I took a long sip. 'And to you two being beautifully behaved children while your Mummy's away.'

'I'm going to miss you, Mumples. Here's to you.' Spring lifted her glass.

'And to Granny,' added Scarlett. 'You must give her our love. I must say that you're a good and dutiful daughter, Mum. A fine example to the two of us.' She lifted her drink too, managing to slop a fair-sized splash down the front of her garment. It was difficult to decide just what she'd come as today. Half of her was ecclesiastical and the other half was connected with the world of Bohemia and high learning. She looked most of all like a Holbein portrait. Of a man.

'Well, 'I said, 'I only hope that when I'm eighty you care for me this way. However difficult I become.'

'No problem, Mumples, you're never going to reach eighty, not leading the life you live.' Scarlett laughed, then said quickly, thinking that she might have upset me, 'Only joking. I shall be very upset if you die.' She'd put on her baby voice. Emotional that I was leaving the house for so long.

'Well, I'm going to have to die some time. But I think that Granny might make it before me. I dread that. You won't find me much fun to live with then.'

'I notice that whenever you go to Wales, even when we were small, you always dwell on death. It's a morbid preoccupation with the Welsh, isn't it?'

'It is, Scarlett.' I picked up the champagne.' For anyone?' They pushed forward their glasses for more, like two cuckoos in a nest.

'The one trouble with you girls,' I said, 'is that you're both very greedy. Had you though of leaving some over for your thirsty old Mum?'

'Not in this bottle,' Spring replied. 'I'm buying some more. My treat, little Mumples.'

'And after that it'll be my treat. I'm buying you a bottle, Mum. Sod the money, my grant comes through on Monday.'

'Champagne,' I said, 'to celebrate my departure from Cheyne Walk. Anybody would think you two were glad to get rid of me.'

'What else – of course!'

'You stupid old cow!'

Yes. I'd miss them as much as they'd miss me. There was no getting around that fact.

Eighteen

'Mama – it's me, Eve.' I stood in the doorway of her bedroom, unable to believe my eyes. She hadn't heard me come in and, even now, wasn't aware that I was in the room. She was unrecognisable to me as my mother. Her teeth were in a glass of water near the wash-basin.

'She won't wear them any more, not unless I cajole her into doing so,' my sister, Edna, had said. I'd been to Edna's house first to say that I'd arrived and to wish them a happy holiday. Now they'd gone and I was alone in the house with my mother. Unless the lodger was in downstairs. 'And it's not worth the upset, so if I were you I wouldn't bother. You'll find that she won't want to get out of her nightie and dressing gown all day either.'

'What, Mama!'

'I know. She's always been a one for dolling herself up. But not any more. You'll find her very changed, Evie. But there's very little anyone can do. She'll enjoy having you down though, she's looking forward to that.'

'I'm looking forward to it, too. I've brought my typewriter down with me so I can get on with a lot of work at the same time. And if I have to do a television show I can pop up to London for the day. She'd be OK for that long, wouldn't she?'

'Oh, yes. The neighbours drop in, and Meals on Wheels call every day so that she has a hot meal at midday. She'll be fine. She mostly sits in the back bedroom, staring into the gas fire and smoking. That's a bit of a worry she'll set fire to herself one day. All her nighties have cigarette burns in them, and the dressing gowns. She's fondest of the red one, she doesn't like that being taken off when it's due to go in the wash. I suppose it's the bright colour. Oh, and don't be upset if you hear her wandering around at night. She

184

likes to keep an odd routine of her own, nothing much to do with night and day as we know it. But she hasn't fallen so far. There are plenty of pieces of furniture to hang onto. The legs have deteriorated quicker than anything. You'll see.'

I was seeing now. Seeing the jaw sagging almost down to the chin, but moving continuously as the shrunken mouth murmured an unintelligible monologue of its own. From the side, the hollowed eyes appeared barely open, the lids shuttered down so that only a faint glimmering line showed that there were eyes in there at all. The hair, that once luxuriant mane, was now sparcely covering the skull. The line of the spine was even more curved, if that was possible, than I'd remembered it from last time I'd seen her, some five months before.

A cigarette dangled limply between her fingers. I watched her raise it towards her mouth, uncertainly, as if unable to find the right place. Not wanting to witness any more, I stepped forward into her line of vision.

'Hello, my darling. Your little baby's arrived.' When I hugged her I did it very gently, she felt so fantastically frail. I was afraid that her brittle bones might break.

It was a month of anguish, exhaustion, impatience, and above all of loneliness. My mother – once my confidante, my companion, and my closest friend, that mother had vanished. She had been replaced by a stranger. A querulous, demanding, irritable old woman. Someone who was living almost totally in the childhood of her past. Not my past, not one in which my sister or myself or my father existed, so that I would have been able to join in with her interminable and incoherent stream of reminiscences. But a world inhabited exclusively by her mother and her father, and her small, adorable self.

'I was a lovely little baby, wasn't I . . . do you remember the lace dress I wore for my sixth birthday . . . it had a pink silk sash to tie around the waist . . . and I kept it for a long time . . . I used to put it on my dolls . . . where are my dolls?' She'd turn in sudden fury to me, suspicious that I, a stranger, had stolen her cherished dolls. Then her mood would become slyly wheedling.

'What I'd like for my birthday party is strawberry jelly

and vanilla blancmange, and I want some now. I want it for breakfast.' She was perpetually hungry, her inner life revolved around food. I couldn't begin to think where it all went to, where it disappeared in her bird-like frame. I seemed to spend the entire time preparing trays for her, all of it kiddies' food. Soft-boiled eggs and strips of buttered toast. Welsh rarebit with all the crusts removed. Cream cakes. Brown bread and butter, sliced thin and spread thickly with blackcurrant jam – though not so much of the blackcurrant jam. She'd complained bitterly of the hard pips, why hadn't I bought plum instead? No sooner had I taken away her tray of dirty dishes to wash up, than she'd be crying out again that she was 'sinking with hunger', and when would tea be ready. She was constantly critical of what I was doing for her, aware only of all the things that I was leaving undone.

Once, running to the shops up in the high street, I left her alone for half an hour. When I returned I found her straddled on the stairs, sobbing. She was starving, she said. She hadn't eaten all day. Before leaving I'd served her a large portion of steamed haddock and poached egg, followed by a bowl of tinned peaches and ice cream. She denied ever having tasted such delights.

I put on almost a stone in weight. My eating company was demanded at every meal, and there were at least six of those a day. She'd take food off her own plate with shaking fingers and transfer it to my own, insisting that I eat it up. Wasting good food was a sin in the eyes of God.

She referred to Our Lord constantly, beseeching him to take her in the night. She prayed aloud to us both, her God in heaven and me, to be re-united with Mamma and Dadda. She never mentioned any reunion with my father though he had resided in heaven for the past twenty-two years too. Once, trying desperately to elevate the drone of the one-sided conversation, I suggested that there was a good chance of coming across my Daddy, as well as her Dadda, up there. They'd be able to date again, and wouldn't that be good fun. But she simply stared at me in bewilderment. I'd been made to feel callous and intentionally cruel. I didn't attempt such desperate jollity again.

But it wasn't like that all the time, and when it was, I felt that hanging on grimly was worth everything for the astounding bouts of lucidity that sometimes surfaced. There was no way of knowing when these would occur. Now and again it was in the middle of the night, at the end of an afternoon, or just before dawn broke over the sea-gull bay.

Twice, it had happened at dawn. I had been awakened by her voice, which happened every night so I was used to it. But this time there was laughter, the lilt of gaiety was present in the conversation she was conducting with herself. The gaiety for which my mother was famous in the family. My senses sharpened through my superficial sleep so that I was out of bed and there with her before I had even finished pulling on my dressing gown. I moved as swiftly as I'd done when I heard my babies crying in their sleep. And I had come to regard living with my mother like this, and caring for her with such concentration, as living with and looking after a child. I was filled with tenderness the whole time. When she drowsed in a chair in front of the television, or lay back on her pillows and started dreaming, I found myself gazing down at her with such overwhelming love and compassion that I had a physical pain around my heart. Despite her cantankerous and often hostile attitude towards me, I felt closer to her than I had ever done in my life. After all, I was only doing for her what she did for me when I'd been a helpless infant. And I felt privileged and humbled to see her so intimately in her infirmity. As if it was an important stage in the lifelong union between us.

The first time the dawn experience had happened I found her, still in her nightie and red dressing gown, but with a hat on her head and a silk scarf tied jauntily around her neck. She was standing in front of the mirror with her teeth in her hands and was trying to fit her top denture into her mouth. She turned, laughing at my approach. Her voice was light and familiar, instead of the usual whine.

'These teeth are going to have to be replaced with a new set – look at how loose they are.' She grinned at me, her eyes dancing. 'How can I go out with this new hat on, and no teeth!'

'I agree, the total effect would look a trifle incongruous, Mama. We must get you some new ones.'

She looked at me sharply. 'Don't be so daft. Where would I be going to anyway. I don't go out any more. My legs don't work – haven't you noticed, Eve?' It was one of the few times that she'd addressed me by name.

'Come on, get a cup of tea on the go. We'll take it and go and sit out on the balcony. I love watching the sun coming up over the bay. It think it is one of the most beautiful sights I have ever seen. Your father used to love it too. Good job he can't see me now, looking like this.' She'd glanced down at her dressing gown. 'I think I'll get out of this old thing today. Put a summer dress on for a change. Could you get the black and white silk one out of the wardrobe for me, Eve, there's a good girl.'

I wept with happiness as I stood out in the kitchen, making the tea. When I returned with it she was already out on the balcony with a blanket wrapped around her for warmth.

'You look awful, Eve. What's the matter? Are you working too hard at all that silly writing, or what? You're not getting any younger, it's time you started to slow down or you won't make old bones. Though what's so special about making old bones I've never understood. Look at me, I'd be better off dead. I want you to promise me, Eve, that when I get senile and I don't make sense any more you'll do the decent thing and give me an overdose. I don't want to be a silly old thing blathering about the place. I'd like to go in a dignified manner, in this house, peacefully lying in that bed. The one I got when your father and I were married. He had such a sense of humour, didn't he, Daddy. He'd have been so proud of you now, if only he'd lived to see it. You get all of your ability from Daddy, you know. All I've ever given you is the will to work. But see to it, Eve, that you're happy. That's important. You don't look happy today to me. You seem to be worrying about something. And I don't like all this weight you've put on. And your hair, what's happened to it? It's two different colours. Black at the end and grey at the roots – you want to get into the hairdresser. They can see to it. The manageress there is Pat now. A very nice girl. Tell her your mother sent you, and that I'll be in for a perm some time next week.' I listened intently, committing everything to memory in this rediscovery of the strong and loving mother I knew.

Two hours later I'd lost her again.

Nineteen

'Yes, it is a great shame we have to leave Venice today. Scarlett and I could stay on, but you see Spring has to be back in the theatre tomorrow night.' We, all three of us, smile dazzlingly at the millionaire. His name is Gregory, his surname sounds German, but he speaks in an American growl. I'm finding him undeniably attractive with two glasses of champagne in me. My hangover has flown away, over the horizon of the shimmering sea of the Lido, up and over the baroque domes of the Excelsior Hotel, into the azure oblivion of the cloudless sky. 'It's so wonderful here, isn't it?' I stretch my tanned legs, slim and shapely after my rigorous pre-holiday diet.

'Mumples! You look hideous, You're so FAT!' Spring's first words to me on my return from my mother's.

'Interesting hair-effect, two-tone.' Spring had inspected my silvered scalp. 'I wonder if Ricci could organise a wig for me like that.'

'Not now, my angels. Your old Mum's not up to criticism of even the loving kind.' But by a week later I was feeling a little bit better, able to joke about myself too.

Now I was on top of the world. The gondolier last night had been a good idea. One should sample the local delights, as I'd said to the girls. After all they'd found their distractions in the disco. The evil hangover, the result of our tour of the gondoliers' bars, was the only bad thing about it all. And now that had disappeared, thanks to Gregory's hospitality. But we'd have to be getting along soon, we had presents to purchase before catching the plane. Spring had to buy four for her London lovers, and Scarlett had still to decide on which Venetian lace frock would look best on her fiancé, the transvestite that she'd got engaged to before we'd come away on holiday. I'd paid for, but still had to collect, the set of Murano glasses which I'd be taking back for Mama. They were in assorted and brilliant primary colours of the rainbow. She'd enjoy them. She'd imagine that they were jewels. And use them to stub out her cigarettes. I'd pop down on the train next weekend and unwrap them for her myself. I was looking forward to watching her childish delight, the clasping of her fingers around their beauty, the exciting clapping of the hands at such a present.

I tell the girls to go and collect their things, I have mine, I am fully dressed. In a wisp of silk, the colour of the sand to show off the depth of my tan.

Gregory leans towards me when they've gone. 'Eve, may I call you by your first name, please? I am not usually so informal on a first meeting, but since now we are so short of time, may I say that you are the most attractive woman that I have met in years. I have been married and divorced three times and in recent years have despaired of feeling as I do now, sitting here with you. I am no longer a young man, you understand, but I feel we were destined to meet. May I call you when I am next in London. I shall be staying at Claridges, in October. I am coming over for an important sale of Egyptian art at Christie's. Maybe you will do me the honour of dining with me . . .'

'Well, Mumples, you've got that old goat hooked then. It could be skiing in Switzerland for us all at Christmas, if you play your cards right.' Spring squeezes my right arm. The plane is about to take off.

'You must ask him to get in a supply of paints and an easel for me. I've never painted a snow scene, I'm rather interested in tonal harmony of white-on-white.' Scarlett opens her *Guide to the Churches of Venice*. 'You know what, Mum, I might take up religion in a big way this winter. I must get some nifty Madonna outfits together.'

I settle back happily between them. The first thing I had to organise when I got back to London was which VD clinic to go to each month. I'd ring old Jake and ask him which was the friendliest, we'd probably start going together. Patience could be at home, making a meal for our return.

Rather a cosy, regular, monthly event.

I smile as the plane soars in the sky. I adore the sensation of soaring.